THE BEAR AFFAIR

THE
BEAR AFFAIR

•

CYNTHIA POWELL

POWELL
c.1

AVALON BOOKS
THOMAS BOUREGY AND COMPANY, INC.
401 LAFAYETTE STREET
NEW YORK, NEW YORK 10003

PRINTED IN THE UNITED STATES OF AMERICA
ON ACID-FREE PAPER
BY HADDON CRAFTSMEN, SCRANTON, PENNSYLVANIA

To Gary—

my beary best friend

Chapter 1

"**Y**ou're in big trouble, Miss Berne."

Taylor Berne met the stern, implacable gaze of Ms. Hardigree, the hospital administrator. "Hard-nosed Hardigree," the nurses called her, and she had earned the title.

"Again?" Taylor asked, her soft brown eyes widening in dismay.

Ms. Hardigree peered over the rims of her stainless steel bifocals and placed one sharp elbow on her massive mahogany desk. "In five minutes," she warned Taylor, "Dr. Kayne Frost is going to march into this office and demand an explanation for your behavior. What do you suggest I tell him?"

Taylor gulped, her normal composure shaken by this unwelcome news. "Tell him I've moved, no forwarding address."

Ms. Hardigree didn't laugh. She flicked an invisible speck from the lapel of her jacket and shot Taylor a look of—could it be sympathy? "It wouldn't work, my dear. Besides, he's furious enough already. We can't afford to antagonize him any further."

Taylor swallowed, battling a wave of nervous apprehension. She'd seen Dr. Frost angry before, with his blue-green eyes as dark as a storm on the ocean. Every time something went wrong, he was there, his mouth tightening to a thin, curved line, his marble face mocking her with cool tolerance. A shiver ran down her spine.

"That mad, is he?" she whispered weakly.

Ms. Hardigree sniffed, fighting back the barest hint of a smile. She patted her no-nonsense hairdo firmly into place, regaining her professional demeanor. "Fit to be tied," she asserted calmly.

Taylor blinked in amazement. There was a definite twinkle in the woman's eye. Maybe Ms. Hardigree wasn't so tough after all. Maybe a sympathetic spirit lay beneath her formidable exterior. There might be some hope after all.

Ms. Hardigree shook one neatly manicured finger at Taylor. "But don't think I'm going to ignore this, this—*problem* between you and Dr. Frost, because I won't." Then her face softened, the severe features relaxing into a mellow expression. "Still, Taylor, no matter what Dr. Frost says, I haven't once regretted my decision to hire you. You've done a fine job managing the hospital gift shop."

Taylor smiled, acknowledging her own small accomplishments. She couldn't perform life-saving surgery, or miraculously cure disease, or even nurse the sick back to health, but in her own unique way she helped the patients and families at Stuart General Hospital.

Ms. Hardigree continued, her chin set in a stubborn line, "When I told the board of directors you were stocking the shop full of Teddy bears, substituting the traditional inventory for a stuffed bear menagerie, well, they were skeptical, to say the least.'' She removed her glasses and lowered her voice to a confidential whisper. ''They're a fussy group—resistant to change of any kind.''

Taylor nodded seriously.

The beginning of a smile curved the sharp corners of Ms. Hardigree's mouth. ''But you've turned the shop into a big attraction. And the families think it's wonderful. After all, a Teddy is the perfect present for a sick relative—child or adult.''

Taylor smiled back in mutual understanding.

''And the patients,'' Ms. Hardigree added, ''adore you. Well, you must see how their faces light up when you push your bear cart through the halls. Of course, the children just love it, but even the elderly patients perk right up when you make your rounds.''

Taylor had seen it many times, the warmth and affection spilling out around the bears, an enchanting kind of spell woven by her furry friends. Teddy bears brought out the best in people, a special kind of love that had its own power of healing. She felt lucky to be a part of it.

Ms. Hardigree's sturdy features broke into a robust grin. ''And your little bear hospital, right inside the gift shop. What a clever idea that was. Children can certainly relate better to their own injuries when their Teddy gets a matching sling or a cast. No wonder they started calling you 'Doc' Berne, the Teddy bear doctor.''

Taylor flushed, her cheeks warm as she remembered

how that nickname had led to certain—complications. But Ms. Hardigree didn't dwell on the matter.

"In short, Taylor Berne, you're a valuable employee. You and those bears of yours have brought magic into Stuart General. Yes, magic. But for someone who's so good with people, it's hard to understand why you don't get along with Dr. Frost." She leaned across the desk, her stark features rigid once again. "So tell me, what seems to be the problem? What *is* it between you two?"

Taylor shifted in her seat, squirming under the direct interrogation. She flipped a short strand of sandy-brown hair from her face and tried to make sense of her feelings for Dr. Kayne Frost. "I'm not sure, Ms. Hardigree," she ventured. "The man is so," she debated a moment, "so difficult!"

Ms. Hardigree leaned a little closer. "In what way?"

Taylor bit her lower lip and chose her words carefully. "Well, I know he's an excellent cardiac surgeon and a great asset to this hospital. He can probably recite medical journals from memory."

Ms. Hardigree continued to stare expectantly.

"And the patients are lucky to have him here," Taylor added with characteristic honesty. "But, Ms. Hardigree, sometimes I wonder if he's really human!"

Ms. Hardigree started to speak, then glanced at the open doorway, her eyes widening.

Taylor continued, warming to the subject. "It's just that Dr. Frost is always so *serious*. He never smiles. He's like some sort of medical machine—making his rounds at dawn, performing surgery all day, studying medical updates in the cafeteria at dinner. No wonder he's lost all sense of feeling. He never does anything but work. Why, I'll bet his idea of a good time is curling up with a bottle of mineral water and the *Physician's Desk Reference*.''

''Miss Berne—'' mumbled Ms. Hardigree, agitated.

''I know,'' Taylor interrupted. ''I shouldn't say these things about him. You probably think he's perfect. But that's just the problem, Ms. Hardigree, he's too perfect. Dr. Frost doesn't have any weaknesses. He can't allow for human error, because he's not human himself. There's icewater in his veins.''

Ms. Hardigree let out a soft moan.

''I'm sorry if this upsets you, Ms. Hardigree, but it's the truth. Frost,'' she mused, her eyes bright and defiant. ''A chilling name. Well, the name fits. What else could you call a man who objects to a few little Teddy bears?''

''It isn't the bears I object to,'' came a low, masculine voice behind her.

Taylor stiffened and sat very still. She didn't have to turn to see who was speaking. Dr. Kayne Frost.

Burning with humiliation, she swiveled slowly in her seat and found herself staring at the great cardiac surgeon himself. Tall and stern, he stood before her. His icy, aquamarine eyes glared down into hers from his much-too-handsome face.

''You're a menace, Miss Berne,'' he continued, folding bare, muscled arms across his broad chest. ''A complication. And I don't like complications.''

Taylor groaned, swearing hotly under her breath. Why, she wondered in helpless frustration, did these things always happen to her? It wasn't fair! Dr. Frost never failed to catch her at her worst. Just once, she would like to prove to him that she was not just a gawking, gift-shop-clerk-out-of-control.

"Now, Dr. Frost," muttered Ms. Hardigree, rising valiantly from the relative safety of her chair, "I—that is—I'm sure we can straighten out this whole matter."

Frost dismissed the suggestion with a single wave of his hand. As he stepped farther into the room, there was a hint of swagger in his walk, a certain angle to his wide shoulders that made Taylor think of a pirate walking the deck of his ship. His lean, sculptured body was not obscured by the surgical scrubs he wore; in fact, every hard curve was clearly defined.

Yes, there was something rakish about Dr. Frost, from the jagged scar on his right hand, to the smooth sinews of his arms, sleek and sun-bronzed. His jet hair, as dark and rich as West Indian spices, feathered back from the strong forehead, an untamed wave falling just above one eye. Where a pirate would have worn a sword, a silver stethoscope uncoiled form his right pocket.

His mouth curved into a slow, mocking smile, the gleaming white teeth smooth and even. "There is a simple cure," he assured Ms. Hardigree, his eyes studying Taylor, making her feel like a contagious disease. "Remove the complication. Keep her in the gift shop and away from me."

Taylor swallowed hard, lifted her eyes, and met his accusing glare without a wince. "I deserve a chance to explain, Dr. Frost. If it's about the bears in the hospital laundry—"

He lifted one dark eyebrow, faintly amused, blatantly skeptical. "Just one more unfortunate incident," he breathed, the careful control evident in his voice, "in a *long* list of similar occurrences. But go ahead and explain, Miss Berne, I'm eager to hear the details. I must admit, I have been curious about the *pink* surgical scrubs."

She stood to face him, her fawn eyes bright and defensive. "How was I to know the dye would run? The labels on the bears clearly said machine washable." She wrung her slender hands together. "Those particular bears were used to decorate the newborn nursery, but they'd gotten a bit dusty. I was only trying to keep them as sanitary as possible. Imagine my surprise when the color washed out of every single bear."

"Imagine mine," Frost countered, "when the scrub suits turned up in—," he took a deep breath, his firm mouth twitching, "—*pale pink*."

"You never let me explain what happened," she insisted. "You see, the machine didn't drain properly, and some of the dye was left at the bottom and, well—"

She stopped and bit her lip. Frost didn't look any calmer now than when the incident had first happened. She remembered his less-than-sympathetic reaction, his cool stare, the unyielding set of his jaw that set her heart hammering in her chest. Perhaps it was better not to remember. "I think you're blaming me unfairly, Dr. Frost. You're still holding a grudge because of the incident in pediatrics."

"Really?" he asked, his voice heavy with sarcasm.

She nodded vigorously. "I had a perfectly good reason for impersonating a doctor."

His eyes flashed with mild interest. "I can't wait to hear it."

"Well, you know the children call me 'Doc' Berne—"

His mouth quirked, the reaction involuntary. "I assure you, I don't have to be reminded."

"Anyway," she continued, her voice eager, "I was 'operating' on one-eyed Bradley—"

He held up his hand. "One-eyed Bradley?"

"Little Merry Worthing's bear," she explained impatiently, "that's what she calls him."

"Of course," he apologized. "How silly of me. But go on. You were giving him a new eye, I suppose?"

She stopped, puzzled. "Oh no, that would spoil his character."

"I see," he choked.

"He needed a paw patching," Taylor informed him, "on the left foot."

"Ah yes, the foot," he nodded, his expression serious.

"But Merry insisted the operation wouldn't work unless I put on a white 'doctor's jacket.' So, you see, I had to."

Dr. Frost stifled a small cough. "Naturally."

Taylor frowned. "I couldn't help it if one of your residents thought I really was a doctor."

Frost let out a heavy sigh. "Miss Berne, didn't you find it a bit unusual when he tried to discuss the case with you?"

She considered this a moment, her expression thoughtful. "Yes—but I explained about the broken foot and the answer seemed to satisfy him. Dr. Frost,

I just didn't realize he thought I meant the girl, not the bear."

Dr. Frost rolled his eyes in quiet exasperation. "*That's* how she ended up in x-ray."

Taylor flinched at the tone of his voice. "Lucky I caught the mistake in time."

Frost reached out and tilted her chin toward him, his strong, cool fingers pressing softly into her skin. "Lucky for you."

The pulse quickened in her throat, electrified by the power of his touch. Taylor backed away, startled by the intensity of her own response. How was it that this skilled surgeon—so proficient with a scalpel, so expert with a needle—how was it that the meticulous Dr. Frost knew how to touch her in the most unscientific way? His experience, apparently, was not entirely academic.

Taylor struggled for the right words. "Yes, well, I hope we can put that episode behind us."

Frost folded both hands behind his back and paced the floor with an easy, restless energy. "We can try, Miss Berne, but I'm afraid the problem won't go away." He stopped and cocked his head, his eyes regarding her as a strict teacher might look upon a naughty child. "Those bears of yours keep popping up like a bad rash."

Taylor shook her head, sending fine, cashmere waves of hair tumbling about her face. "You're exaggerating."

He tilted his brow, eyeing her uncertainly. "Am I? What about the chocolate bears you gave out last week? My patients aren't allowed any food the night before their surgery."

She nodded. "The nurses explained all that to me. I was very careful about who I gave the candy to."

"Uh-huh," he muttered with a look of stern reproof. "But, in spite of your efforts, Flora Mills was caught with three empty wrappers."

Taylor cringed. He was right, of course. Flora had consumed several of the chocolate Teddies before the nurses found the incriminating evidence. But the incident wasn't entirely her fault. Flora had a decided fondness for anything chocolate.

"She confessed to sneaking the candy off my cart," Taylor protested.

Frost's aqua eyes widened. "Fortunately, we were able to discover the problem. But if it had been an emergency . . . "

"Please, Dr. Frost," Ms. Hardigree interrupted. "Nothing really bad has happened. Miss Berne may be a bit, oh, exuberant, but you're overlooking her finer qualities."

Dr. Frost rested his hands on his hips. "Which are?"

"Well," intoned Ms. Hardigree, ready to enumerate Taylor's relative merits, "she has many, many . . . " She paused, thinking rapidly. "Such as—" Her brow wrinkled painfully.

Frost waited expectantly.

At a temporary loss for words, Ms. Hardigree retreated behind her bifocals. The seconds ticked by in agonizing silence.

"Oh yes!" exclaimed Ms. Hardigree, rebounding with unexpected fervor. "She's very well liked." Triumphant, she folded her arms across her chest.

"So I've heard," Frost told her, a wry smile on his

lips. "But the more stories I hear about *Doctor* Berne and the 'magic' power of her Teddy bears, the more it makes me wonder."

His eyes scanned Taylor, assessing her with a brief sardonic glance. "Can this be the same Taylor Berne who kidnapped the geriatrics patients, wheeling them out onto the lawn for a Teddy bear picnic?" He glared at her with open disapproval. "The day nurses were frantic. Misplacing patients is no small matter, Miss Berne."

Taylor dropped her gaze. "I felt very badly about that. A small communication error. One of the volunteers forgot to relay my message. Besides, I didn't actually abduct any patients. I just borrowed them for a while."

Kayne turned back to Ms. Hardigree. "Magic is it? I'd call it voodoo. Miss Berne should come with a label attached—**Warning: any contact with this woman could be hazardous to your health**."

"Really, Dr. Frost," scolded Ms. Hardigree. "You're being very rough on the girl. In fact, I haven't had a single complaint about her from anyone but you." She rubbed her chin and looked thoughtfully from Dr. Frost to Taylor. "Strange," she mumbled, "that she should have this effect only on you."

"Is it true, Miss Berne?" demanded Dr. Frost. "Do you reserve this special treatment for me alone? Is there something about me you don't like? Something other than my *inhuman* qualities?"

Taylor's honey-brown eyes filled with confusion. She took a long, hard look at Kayne Frost. What was it about this man that she found so disturbing?

"He's gorgeous," said a mischievous voice inside her. A stunning specimen of male beauty as flawless as an anatomy drawing. But, of course, her interest was purely clinical.

She looked away. "Of course, I don't *dislike* you Dr. Frost."

"I'm relieved to hear it," he murmured, a hint of mockery in his voice.

Ms. Hardigree continued to study them. "Something's got to be done."

Dr. Frost narrowed his eyes. "I agree completely."

Taylor folded her arms across her chest and sank back into the chair. "So do I."

Ms. Hardigree looked approvingly from one to the other. "Good!" she exclaimed. "We're making progress. You both agree." She rubbed her hands together. "Now, to get the ball rolling . . . "

Dr. Frost's beeper sounded and the sudden noise startled Taylor out of her seat.

Dr. Frost studied her curiously. "Jumpy, aren't we?"

"I can't stand those things," she insisted.

He frowned. "The patient who needs me right now might disagree with you."

Taylor flushed with shame. It was true. The pager was a useful tool in modern medicine, a valuable instrument that could summon any doctor at a moment's notice. But those relentless beeps could cause their own brand of suffering. "Sorry, I—"

Dr. Frost shrugged. "Never mind. I don't have time for any more explanations." He turned impatiently to

Ms. Hardigree. "I assume you'll handle the—" he glanced at Taylor, "—the problem?"

Ms. Hardigree followed him to the door, doing her best to assure his speedy exit. "Don't worry, Dr. Frost. I'll take care of everything."

Frost nodded with satisfaction and left to answer the call.

Taylor turned to Ms. Hardigree, her stomach sinking. "So what happens now? Are you going to—" she swallowed, her insides queasy, "—fire me?"

Ms. Hardigree's eyes widened to the size of saucers. "Nonsense, girl. The thought never even crossed my mind. Besides, we need you around here."

"But Dr. Frost—"

Ms. Hardigree smiled enigmatically, oblivious to Taylor's warning. "A charming man, Dr. Frost. Wants only the best for his patients. He's trained a crackerjack operating team, uses all the latest equipment—when he can get it. This year Dr. Frost wants a new echo-cardiogram machine—an expensive addition to his collection, but very worthwhile." She sank slowly into her chair, settling her ample frame comfortably against the executive cushions. "It could take some convincing, but I think Dr. Frost may see the merit of your work as well."

Taylor doubted it, but she decided not to argue.

Still smiling, Ms. Hardigree studied Taylor. "He's a bachelor, you know."

Taylor wrinkled her brow. "Yes, I've heard the nurses mention that he's single."

Ms. Hardigree's smile widened to a Cheshire cat

grin. "There's not a woman in this hospital who hasn't had a second look at our Dr. Frost."

Taylor was well aware of the hospital gossip about Kayne Frost. Thirty-five, handsome and available, the dream of every marriage-pushing mother, every meddling matchmaker. But Dr. Frost continued to frustrate them all. Dedicated to his job, devoted to his work, he was far too busy for a serious relationship. He remained loyal to his stethoscope.

But Taylor would sooner marry a frog than a physician. She'd had enough experience with workaholic doctors to last a lifetime. Not for her, the lonely nights spent waiting with a cooling dinner and a rising temper. That unhappy scenario was all too familiar. She'd seen it happen to her mother. It would not happen to her.

Ms. Hardigree cut into her thoughts. "I suppose you've noticed it too," she suggested. "Dr. Frost is a very attractive man."

Gorgeous, Taylor amended silently.

"And you, Taylor, you're a pretty enough young woman. How old are you, dear, about twenty-four?"

Taylor nodded, suspicious. "Ms. Hardigree, you're not suggesting—" she hesitated. No. Even Ms. Hardigree could see there wasn't the slightest attraction between herself and Dr. Frost. She stopped. Okay, maybe a little attraction on her part. But, even though her experience with men was limited, she recognized the feelings for what they were—purely physical.

After all, Dr. Frost kept himself in prime condition. All those raw vegetables and protein shakes he consumed in the cafeteria had not gone to waste. And the hours spent in the hospital gym—he'd invested them well. His body—an inspiration to the physical therapists—was a lean, mean, operating machine.

No wonder she responded like an adolescent schoolgirl. But despite that response, Dr. Frost was not her type at all. They were completely incompatible. He dealt strictly with science and statistics, with facts and formulas. Taylor believed in feelings as well as facts, in sweet words and sympathy. She was firmly convinced that love and her Teddy bears could help to heal many wounds.

"Never mind, dear," Ms. Hardigree murmured, turning to the view from her large picture window. She stared across the sparkling St. Lucie River to the lush tropical landscape beyond. "Just the ramblings of an old lady."

Taylor followed her gaze. White-winged herons skimmed the air, floating on a Florida breeze. A sailboat drifted by, its painted canvas unfurled to catch the wind coming in from the Atlantic. It was hard to imagine that in the northern states, it was snowing.

Ms. Hardigree turned back. "I suppose this romantic setting is giving me some strange ideas. Besides, I'm sure you and Dr. Frost can start this affair without me."

Taylor stared at her in shock. "Excuse me?"

"Oh, beg your pardon," exclaimed Ms. Hardigree, her cool composure ruffled. "I meant *end* this affair. Yes, put an end to this unfortunate affair." She smiled, beaming. "And I'm going to do everything I can to help."

"Thank you," Taylor mumbled, "for your support." *I think*, she added silently.

Ms. Hardigree pressed on. "Now, as long as I have you here, I might as well tell you that the hospital board is very interested in your 'bear therapy' ideas."

Taylor's heart leapt, and her spirits soared once again. "They are?"

Ms. Hardigree chuckled at Taylor's display of enthusiasm. "Don't look so surprised. You've already demonstrated the beneficial effects of Teddy bears on frightened, lonely patients. But the board would like to hear more of the specifics before granting your request for additional funding."

"Of course," Taylor agreed cheerfully. Nothing could stop her now. "When?"

"Let me see." Ms. Hardigree skimmed her desk calendar, her finger searching for the exact date. "Yes, here it is. You're scheduled for the December meeting, just two days after Christmas." She penciled a simple notation in the appropriate time block, eased back in her seat and tucked the pencil behind her ear. "That gives you seven weeks to prepare."

Taylor leaned forward, the conviction strong in her voice. "I'll be ready, Ms. Hardigree. I'm going to convince them to donate a free bear to every sick child in this hospital."

"I hope so," Ms. Hardigree told her. "Your 'Bear Care' plan is a worthy cause."

Sincere emotion flared in Taylor's warm, brown eyes. "If you could see what a difference it makes to the children," she shook her head, remembering. "In fact, if every member of that board could see, they wouldn't have the heart to say no."

Ms. Hardigree folded her hands, resting them precisely on the edge of her desk. "You've got pluck, Taylor, true determination. But you're going to need every ounce of that determination, and a little grit besides, to get a unanimous vote from the board."

Taylor frowned, somewhat confused. "But you said they're interested. . . . "

Ms. Hardigree pursed her mouth, marring the perfectly drawn lines of cherry-red lipstick. "Interested, yes, but still undecided. Remember, you've got to persuade *all* the board members, including the tough ones. Don't forget Kiki Vandemere."

How could she forget about Kiki? The diamond-encrusted divorcée was difficult to please. She didn't much care for Teddy bears unless they were very rare or very valuable. But even Kiki would come around with some diplomatic persuasion. As for the other undecided board members, well, Taylor would help them decide.

Ms. Hardigree continued. "*Most* of the members support your efforts wholeheartedly."

Taylor cleared her throat, vaguely disturbed. "Most?"

Ms. Hardigree looked away, taking a sudden interest in a small, dark speck on the ceiling. "Well, you may not be aware of this, but we've recently elected a new member to the hospital board." She glanced at Taylor, gauging her reaction.

"Go on," Taylor urged, a shadow of alarm creeping through her.

Ms. Hardigree took a deep breath. "Dr. Martin retired last month," she explained carefully, "leaving an empty position on the board."

As casually as she could manage, Taylor asked, "Yes?"

Ms. Hardigree kept her voice even, her tone matter-of-fact. "And it is customary to have at least one board member from the medical staff."

The medical staff. Meaning one of the doctors. Taylor blinked in shock. No. It couldn't be.

"Who?" she squeaked.

"Dr. Kayne Frost," responded Ms. Hardigree, a sympathetic smile on her face. "But don't worry, you'll change his mind about the bears. In fact, you might change his mind about a lot of things."

Chapter 2

"**B**oy, this is delicious." Nita Nichols rolled her twinkling dark eyes and sampled another steaming bite from the bubbling pot of gumbo on her stove. "I'm a better cook than I thought."

Taylor suppressed a smile and filled the mismatched cups, mugs, and glasses on the kitchen table with water. She wasn't exactly a guest in Nita's home, after all—more like one of the family—and since her best friend had graciously invited her for dinner, she intended to make herself useful. "Where do you keep the napkins, Nita?"

Nita scoffed and tossed her long auburn braid over one shoulder. "Napkins!" she exclaimed as if Taylor had just told an outrageously funny joke. "My kids need more protection than just plain, ordinary napkins." She retrieved a roll of paper towels from the cupboard and handed it to Taylor. "Here," she said, "we use the extra-strength, double-duty, jumbo-sized, spill-slurping, super-duper brand." She spread her hands wide. "What else could a family of five ask for?"

As if on cue, Nita's three children tore through the

19

narrow kitchen, chasing after a small black streak that darted under the table and shot down the hall, barreling for parts unknown. Taylor knew the streak to be Mittens, running as fast as his white-booted cat-feet would carry him.

"Stop!" Nita yelled. "Enough!" And she fearlessly threw a body-block in front of the racing children.

They skidded to a halt, their untied tennis shoes squeaking in discord against the linoleum floor. "Gee, Mom," the mop-headed Katie protested, her advanced age of seven making her the acknowledged spokesperson for the group, "We were only trying to get Josh's ball back for him."

Three-year-old Josh, whose hair hadn't entirely come in yet, nodded solemnly to his mother. With his pudgy little belly and receding hairline, he reminded Taylor of a miniature Buddha.

Lily, the quiet middle child, folded her arms across her chest and clamped her jaw shut, which didn't surprise anyone. In times of stress, Lily always refused to say anything.

"Enough," their harried mother repeated, "is enough. Josh has a pile of toys in his room. He doesn't need to play with the cat's toy as well." Nita gave them each an affectionate swipe on the head. "Now get back out there and visit with your father until dinner is ready."

Obediently, they shuffled out into the next room. Taylor couldn't help laughing. "Your family's priceless, Nita. Thanks for letting me be a part of it."

"Don't be ridiculous," Nita scolded. "The kids

think of you as their favorite aunt. You've been around since Lily was in diapers.''

Taylor made a face, laughing. ''I can still remember changing some of those diapers.''

Nita's eyes took on a dreamy expression. ''She was a beautiful baby, wasn't she?''

Taylor grinned. ''The most beautiful ever.''

Nita gave her an admonishing glance. ''Just wait until you have one of your own. You'll think yours is the most beautiful ever, too.''

''Probably,'' Taylor agreed, curiously considering that possibility. A baby of her own. She would like more than just one, actually. An only child, Taylor had always envied friends who came from larger families. That was probably why she was drawn to Nita and her crazy, happy crew.

The irrepressible homemaker and her accountant husband, Eric, seemed so happy together, so comfortable, the way she had always imagined a family *should* be. The way her family had never been.

''So how's your father these days, Taylor?''

Nita's questions cut into her thoughts. ''Oh, fine,'' she responded. ''He seems to like Ft. Lauderdale pretty well since he retired. He just moved into a new highrise condo.''

Nita, always mothering, gave her a searching glance. ''Do you miss him?''

Miss him? No, she'd gotten over that long ago. She'd been used to his frequent absences since childhood. That was the flip side of having a doctor for a father. The lonely side. ''Not too much,'' she responded truthfully.

Nita's curious gaze scanned her face again. "So what's up, Taylor? You look preoccupied tonight."

Realizing any form of concealment was useless against Nita's intuition, Taylor explained the harrowing events of the day. She described the unfortunate scene in Ms. Hardigree's office, then summed it up in one word. One harsh, cold syllable that she knew Nita would instantly understand. "Frost," she muttered.

Nita dropped her stirring spoon into the pot. "Oh, Taylor," she whispered in sympathy, "not again."

"Yes," Taylor answered with stoic acceptance, "*again.*"

Nita shook her head in amazement. "What happened this time?"

Taylor made a small grimace. "Does it really matter? The man's impossible. In his eyes, I can't do anything right."

Nita wrinkled her brow. "It is a rather sticky situation."

"Getting stickier by the minute," Taylor added, explaining further about Frost's recent election to the hospital board.

Nita shook her head and was about to reply when three little heads peeped around the edge of the door. "Is dinner ready yet?" Katie asked.

Nita suddenly remembered the spoon in the stove pot and wielded a long-handled fork to fish it out. "Almost, kids," she responded. "Tell your father five more minutes."

Josh's eyes lighted on Taylor and he gave her a

toothy grin. "Ice cream?" he asked, in his most persuasive three-year-old voice.

Taylor smiled back. "Not before dinner, Josh, but if you're a very good boy, I'll take you to the ice cream shop soon."

Josh grinned wider, and the door shut once more.

Nita turned back to Taylor. "And if he's not a good boy?"

Taylor gave her friend a wry smile. "I'll take him anyway, of course."

Nita grinned and continued stirring the gumbo. "Speaking of bad boys—Taylor, it's hard for me to believe that Frost is such a monster. Have you tried reasoning with him?"

Taylor shook her head. "He won't listen to reason. He won't even stand still long enough to let me try."

Nita ladled the piping hot concoction into six heaping bowls. "There has to be a way. And if there is, Taylor, you're the one to think of it." She drew in a deep breath and bellowed sweetly to her family, "Dinner!"

Nita was right, Taylor admitted silently as she sat down to enjoy her meal. If she really put her mind to it, she *could* win Frost to her side. But how?

Taylor fought back a yawn as she unlocked the sliding glass entrance to the hospital gift shop. Her eyes were barely open, but at least her stomach wasn't growling. She'd eaten enough gumbo last night to last a week.

She wouldn't officially open the store for another two hours, but by arriving this early in the morning, she could make her rounds with the bear cart and not leave the shop unattended.

She went through the motions of her morning ritual, carefully checking the contents of the battered cart. A dignified trio of older bears rode on top: Franklin, Almost-Handsome Henry, and Arm-in-a-Sling Alvin. Next to that distinguished company sat a far less reputable bunch: Shad the Shabbiest, along with Pinkie and Lavender, Muff and Tuff. In spite of their much-mended, patchwork appearance, or perhaps because of it, these old favorites were always a hit in geriatrics.

On the bottom of the cart sat the newer bears, the smaller, fluffier, rounder ones with safety eyes and washable bodies. These were designed with children in mind, so no amount of tugging by little hands or gnawing of little teeth could pull off an eye or an ear. These bears were brave, ready to take any punishment in the line of duty.

At the front of the cart, in the place of honor, rested Mr. Marmalade, Taylor's own childhood bear. Wise and wonderful, he stared solemnly back at her, his boot-button eyes reflecting a good humor acquired over three generations.

Taylor rubbed her hand lovingly over his silky, golden fur, noting how the color had mellowed with age, growing warm and luminous like a fine old brandy. His bright-eyed grin, once store-new, had been rubbed away to a wistful smile. There was a certain charm about his aging features, a timeless quality with the beauty and character of an old master painting.

To her, he was a work of art, but to most people,

Mr. Marmalade was just a Teddy bear. Just a lumpy sack of sawdust with a mangy mohair coat and a pair of shoe-button eyes that had long ago lost their luster. But Taylor wasn't bothered by his fading fur, his worn-out seams, or the way his stuffing had settled over the years so that he leaned a little to the left. His value did not diminish in her eyes because of a few imperfections.

In fact, every patch and scar bore meaningful testimony to his bravery, like the crayon mark she'd drawn on his cheek the day he'd played an Indian. She'd dragged him along on all her many adventures, so a bandage covered his right paw where the fur was worn down to the warp and fibers. Even his woolly black nose was partly gone, kissed away during the long, dark nights he'd spent with her in a sterile hospital bed.

Those nights when she'd been sick with asthma, sick and scared and lonely, Mr. Marmalade had kept her safe. He'd made all the difference between relative security and sheer terror, comforting her with that sweet, knowing smile, cuddling her with his fuzzy arms and a warm bear hug. Now, through her work, Taylor had a chance to share that comfort with other children.

But she needed the approval of the hospital board. And without the endorsement of Dr. Frost, she didn't stand a chance.

Convincing Kayne Frost of anything would be a challenge. Trying to persuade the skeptical surgeon that a bunch of Teddy bears could be of medical significance—well, it might be impossible. He'd sooner believe that the moon was made of green cheese.

Still, she had to convince him. If only a few children could feel the safety and comfort from the hug of a Teddy bear, then all her efforts would be worthwhile.

Taylor pushed her cart out the door, the soft steady rhythm of the wheels announcing the progress of her rag-tag collection through the sanitary halls of Stuart General.

She stopped outside the room of the infamous Mitzy Pearl, the five-year-old terror of the east wing. Taylor had never met the little girl, but if advance reports were correct, this child had the hostile disposition of a dictator and the surly manners of a swamp monster. Ms. Hardigree was convinced that Taylor could tame the spoiled creature with the aid of her bears, making Mitzy's hospital stay more tolerable for everyone.

Taylor took a deep breath, wrinkling her nose at the strong, familiar smell of disinfectant. She pushed her cart through the open doorway, then stopped abruptly. Dr. Frost stood inside the room, talking quietly with Mitzy. Taylor waited unobserved, curious to see how Frost would handle this unruly patient.

The little slip of a girl lying quietly on the bed didn't appear to be monstrous at all. With pretty blue eyes, round and wide behind trembling lashes, she looked more frightened than ferocious. But Taylor was more surprised by Dr. Frost's expression. He was smiling.

That warm, white smile hit Taylor broadside. She'd expected Frost to be stern with his patients, especially with this miniature mischief-maker. Instead, he appeared to be calm and compassionate. Even when the child balked at the stethoscope, pulling it roughly from his neck, Frost simply ruffled her hair, managing to distract her and complete his examination without further incident.

Unfortunately, when he turned and saw Taylor, his expression changed from tolerant amusement to controlled courtesy.

"Good morning, *Doctor* Berne," he said, recovering smoothly from his momentary surprise. "Will you be joining us for morning rounds?"

Taylor shook her head and turned to go. "Of course not. If you'll excuse me, Dr. Frost, I'll come back to visit the patient some other time."

Coward, she scolded herself, beating a hasty retreat into the hall. But safely away from Dr. Frost's cynical stare she started breathing a bit easier.

"Not so fast, Miss Berne," a silky voice called from inside the room. "Wait right there."

She smothered a groan and pulled the cart to a halt. What now?

Frost cornered her in the hall, reaching her in seconds with long, purposeful strides. "We need to talk."

Taylor took a few steps backward, dragging the cart along with her. Its wobbling wheels squeaked a protest of their own. "I'm in a bit of a hurry," she explained. She took another stumbling step backward. "Can it wait?"

Frost placed one impeccably-shod foot on the far wheel of her cart, effectively halting her progress. "No," he answered simply, in a deadly calm voice that brooked no argument, "it can't."

Taylor reached out to steady the precarious rocking of the cart, but lost her balance in the process. Grabbing for the nearest handhold, she caught the edge of the cart, dumping several bears on the way. Frost put out a hand to catch her but got an armful of Teddy bears instead. One fragile, moth-eaten seam gave way, covering the doctor's pristine white lab coat with a fine layer of sawdust stuffing.

He coughed hoarsely, trying to clear his throat of the dusty cloud that was settling around him. Taylor saw the conflict raging within him—the steely determination to keep a flaring temper under control, battling against an equally strong desire to laugh. She took a step toward him, sweeping her hands across his coat in a desperate attempt to brush away the unsightly debris.

He clamped his hand over her slender wrist. "Don't move," he said, "don't speak, don't even breathe."

Taylor froze, uncomfortably aware of her precarious situation.

Brushing the dust from his face with one free hand, Frost regained a measure of composure and led her into an empty room nearby. Still holding her in a grip as hard as surgical steel, he brought his face within inches of hers. "You scare me, Taylor Berne," he confessed, staring into her eyes.

Taylor shrugged to hide her confusion. Dr. Frost, scared of her? She could have sworn it was the other way around.

"Your behavior defies all scientific explanation," he continued, his breath warm against her face. "And when I can't explain something, it makes me very cautious.''

Cautious. The way a predator is watchful of its prey. ''It was an accident, Dr. Frost,'' she whispered, her heart hammering with a strange excitement.

His cool aqua eyes watched her closely, the disconcerting scrutiny tightening the knot in her stomach. If the analytical Dr. Frost took her pulse right now, he would wonder if she was in shock. The source of her symptoms had nothing to do with illness, rather the intoxicating side-effects were a direct result of his touch. That interesting discovery would probably shock him to the core of his scientific soul.

As if he, too, felt the effects of some stimulating drug, Frost released her abruptly, shaking his head. ''You're a walking accident,'' he sighed hoarsely.

Taylor rubbed her wrist where he had been holding it, not because of any discomfort she felt, but because her hand was unnaturally warm. ''Sorry about your coat,'' she murmured, making one last attempt to brush it free of sawdust.

Frost signaled her to stay back. ''Forget it,'' he managed, quickly unbuttoning the jacket before she could ''help'' any further. He shed the coat easily, giving Taylor a rare glimpse of the man beneath the professional uniform.

He looked equally forbidding in an immaculately starched shirt and tie. Taylor swallowed, her heart still beating double-time. ''I really am sorry about the jacket, Dr. Frost. I'll be happy to deliver it to the hospital laundry. I'm sure they can wash it in no time, and . . . ''

"No, thank you," Frost returned, shuddering visibly at the suggestion. "You see, I prefer a *white* lab coat."

Taylor winced at the barb. "Of course, but I was just trying—"

"Please, Miss Berne," he cautioned. "*Don't* try. If we're going to be working together, you have to promise *not* to try so hard."

Taylor frowned, blinking with confusion. "Working together?" she asked, somewhat shaken. "Did I hear you correctly, Dr. Frost?"

Frost studied her, a curious expression on his face. "You do that very well, Miss Berne, the innocent act. But you don't have to bat your eyes at me. Ms. Hardigree's already convinced me to cooperate with you."

"She has?" Taylor asked, wondering with sudden anxiety what Ms. Hardigree had been up to since their last meeting.

Frost shook his head in amazement, a gleam of interest in his ocean-blue eyes. "Tell me, Miss Berne, what did you do to her? Cast a spell of some sort? Maybe spill some of your pixie dust on her clothes?"

He shook his jacket for effect, sending a small puff of sawdust swirling into the air between them.

Taylor shot him an indignant look.

Frost gave an impatient shrug and leaned casually against the door frame. "She really believes all that magic mumbo jumbo about you. Nevertheless, I've agreed to study the effects of your bears on my patients."

Taylor narrowed her eyes. "Why? What changed your mind?"

He rolled the dusty jacket into a tight bundle. "Let's

just say Ms. Hardigree has earned my loyalty. I appreciate her tireless campaigning for my new echocardiogram.''

Ms. Hardigree was no fool. She knew the quickest way to Dr. Frost's heart was through high-tech hospital equipment. With Hardigree's support, the echocardiogram remained the pet project of the hospital's holiday ball. Now it was Frost's turn to show his gratitude.

He smiled narrowly. ''In two months,'' he informed Taylor, ''I intend to give a full report to the hospital board regarding your 'Bear Care' program. That should give me enough time to make a thorough study of your methods. Until then,'' he warned, his voice a velvet whisper, ''we'll be working very closely together.''

''Together?'' Taylor asked in shock.

''Together,'' Frost confirmed with unnerving finality. ''Someone has to keep an eye on you, Taylor Berne. If only to protect the patients!''

Katie, Lily, and Josh marched single file up to the deli ice cream counter and pressed their noses longingly against the glass case, staring wide-eyed at the forty mouth-watering flavors. Taylor glanced nervously at her watch. Her lunch hour was almost over, and there was barely enough time for the children to make their selections before Nita arrived to pick them up again.

''Okay, kids,'' she said, trying to encourage a speedy transaction. ''What'll it be this week? Rocky Road? Peppermint Pistachio? How about some Mocha Jamocha?''

She smiled to herself, waiting for the same, in-

evitable results. Every week she brought the kids to
lunch here, giving Nita a free hour to herself, and
every week they picked the same flavor of ice cream
for desert.

"Chocolate!" they all cried in unison.

Taylor grinned and nodded to the red-cheeked, robust man behind the counter. "Three chocolate cones,
please," she told him, "and one vanilla cream," she
added, casting a rebellious glance at the kids. No doubt
they thought she was crazy, but she had her own favorite flavor as well.

"Let's eat outside," she suggested, motioning to
the umbrella-shaded table just beyond the window. The
restaurant was crowded with lunch hour business from
the Stuart General staff next door, and Taylor wanted
to escape the noise and bustle.

Josh gripped his cone carefully between fat little
fingers as they made their way outside. Just as they
settled down at the table and started the race between
the melting ice cream and their slurping tongues, Lily
looked up at Taylor and gave her a small, pleading
look.

"I'm thirsty," she complained.

"Hold my cone for a sec," Taylor told her, "and
I'll get you a cup of water."

Lily balanced both cones in her hands and looked
anxiously down at them. "Hurry," she warned, "before it all melts."

Taylor didn't argue with the straight, simple logic,
but hurried inside and immediately procured a paper
cup. But there was a line at the water fountain and an

even longer one at the counter, and it was several minutes before she made it outside again.

"Hurry!" Lily squeaked, "Oh, Taylor, hurry! It's melting!"

Two small puddles of ice cream formed on the table, one under each of Lily's sticky, dripping arms. "Oh, Lily!" Taylor laughed, relieving the child of both leaking cones. "I'm sorry! Katie, run inside and get some extra napkins while I try to clean this up."

Katie, who had just finished her ice cream, darted away obediently. Josh, his face and hands covered with dark, gooey chocolate, giggled joyfully as Taylor made a futile attempt to scrape the excess ice cream from the rim of each soggy cone. Lily wrinkled her forehead with anxiety and called out another warning. "It's leaking out the bottom, now!"

Taylor tried to plug the small but persistent holes at the bottom of each cone, but crushed one fragile shell instead, dumping an oozing blob of vanilla cream across the front of her thin, pink blouse.

Josh laughed gleefully. Lily stared, aghast. "Oh, never mind," Taylor laughed, abandoning her cone to the trash can and handing Lily her chocolate one to manage as best she could. "It'll come out."

Katie returned, proudly bearing one miserably small, painfully thin napkin. "Thanks, Kate," Taylor said, still smiling. "It's not the super-duper brand your mom uses, but it'll have to do. Lily, hand me the water, please."

Taylor dipped the corner of her napkin into the cup and dabbed it across the front of her blouse. "That's

better already,'' she said cheerfully, working indus-
triously at the spot.

Josh clapped his hands together with happy enthusiasm, accidentally knocking the cup from Taylor's
hand and splashing the remaining water across her
chest. Taylor sighed in resignation. ''Well, I think most
of the ice cream's disappeared anyway,'' she said
glancing down at her soaked, dripping shirt.

Two car doors slammed in the parking lot, and as
the children turned to look, Taylor followed their gaze.
Frowning, she noted a sleek, red Jaguar with *Kiki*
spelled out in bold, embossed letters across the license
plate. A man and a woman left the car and walked
toward her across the shimmering, sun-warmed pave-
ment.

Taylor gasped in momentary panic, praying silently
that Nita would swoop by in her rickety, rust-colored
station wagon and whisk her away before the couple
came any closer. She couldn't think of anyone she
wanted to see less at this moment than Kiki Vandemere,
the still-fabulous-at-forty hospital board member, leaning delicately on the arm of Dr. Kayne Frost.

Taylor had managed to avoid Frost for the past two
days, but there wasn't a chance of avoiding him now.
She forced her attention away from the parking lot and
tried to concentrate on removing the layers of chocolate
from Josh's face.

Kiki's stiletto heels clicked sharply against the side-
walk. She was nearly to the door of the restaurant and
would have swept inside if Frost hadn't paused, then
stopped suddenly. From the corner of her eye, Taylor

could see him staring. She increased her ministrations on Josh's face.

"Ow!" he protested.

Taylor watched Frost shake his head as if clearing it of some disturbing thought, then reach for the door.

Lily, who rarely spoke of her own volition, of course chose *this* moment to turn conversational.

"Taylor," she said in a strong, clear voice, "Is your shirt all better now?"

Taylor swore quietly under her breath.

"I thought I recognized you, Miss Berne," Frost said, forcing Taylor to look up at him. He let his gaze sweep over the table, taking in the sticky, smiling children, the small ice cream puddles, and the long trail of ants that had come to feast on the droppings. He raised an eyebrow and continued in a voice of faint amusement. "Having a picnic?"

Taylor felt her face growing warm, but she squeezed Josh's little hand for support and lifted her chin. "Just finishing our lunch."

Frost's eyes flickered as his stare dropped to the front of her soaked and soggy blouse. "Ice cream?" he asked coolly.

"Vanilla cream," Katie supplied.

"Ah," Kayne nodded, moving his gaze to meet Taylor's eyes. "My favorite flavor."

Kiki, carefully observing this exchange, interrupted frigidly. "Really, Kayne," she said, pointing to her diamond-studded watch, "if we don't hurry, we'll never get a table."

Taylor glanced involuntarily at the dark-haired, velvet-eyed Kiki. Cold, green gems glinted off her ears and throat, flashing brilliantly in the sun. The large, vividly colored stones coordinated perfectly with the custom-tailored outfit she wore. As usual, Kiki looked as if she'd just been photographed for a fashion magazine. And Taylor looked like a perfect subject for the 'don't' column.

"You go ahead," Frost suggested. "Get us a table, I'll be right in."

Without a backward glance, Kiki strolled into the restaurant. Taylor turned to Dr. Frost and gave him a speculative stare. She wasn't surprised to see him with Kiki, just a bit disappointed. It was common knowledge throughout the hospital grapevine that Kiki had just divorced husband number three, but Taylor had thought Frost, of all people, would be immune to the woman's matrimonial schemes.

Or maybe Frost was playing his own game. As a fellow member of the hospital board, Kiki would be a strong ally for him. And Dr. Frost would go to any lengths to get his new echocardiogram machine. He'd agreed to put up with the bears, hadn't he? Even if it was only temporary. Maybe he was willing to put up with Kiki as well.

Taylor watched through the restaurant window where the svelte, satin-suited Kiki regally requested a table. *What man wouldn't want to put up with Kiki?* she asked herself truthfully.

Katie glanced up at Dr. Frost shyly. "Are you having ice cream, too?"

He gave her a quick smile. "I might."

Not likely, Taylor thought in silent mutiny. Kiki would never approve of the mess. "Don't let us keep you,'' Taylor said. Her tone was more sarcastic than she'd intended.

Frost narrowed his eyes. "I won't. I wanted to advise you, Miss Berne, that I'll be reviewing my schedule soon," he paused, "to see when I can fit you in."

Taylor resisted the urge to shake him by his far-too-broad shoulders. Instead, she smiled benignly. "I'm available most mornings, Dr. Frost."

He grinned in spite of himself. "I'll keep that in mind."

From inside the restaurant, Kiki curved one perfectly manicured finger at Frost and motioned him to follow.

"Later, Miss Berne," he said, and turned to answer the summons.

"Hmph!" Taylor snorted indignantly.

"Hmph!" the children repeated and burst into giggles.

Taylor turned down one of Nita's frequent invitations to visit and spent the weekend in virtual seclusion. For the first time in years, she felt a void that her substitute family couldn't fill. To keep her mind off a vague, lonely feeling, she kept herself busy, catching up on chores around her apartment.

On Monday morning, she was back at work, too busy to think about anything except her customers. But the afternoon traffic was slow, and she was left alone with only her troubled thoughts for company. She turned up the volume on her dancing clock-radio bear, hoping that the soothing strains of music would distract her troubled thoughts. The fuzzy fabric-covered Teddy moved in slow synchronization with the easy-listening melody.

She hummed along with the pleasant little tune, propping her feet on a nearby stool. The dancing radio bear moved his arms in a gentle arc, swiveling his legs in time to the barely perceptible beat. Taylor followed his comfortable swaying, temporarily mesmerized by the predictable, mechanical motions. If only Dr. Frost were that predictable. Then she might be able to understand him and understand her own reaction to him. So far, she hadn't any luck in that area at all.

The encounter at the deli, well, she'd rather not think about that. But the scene she'd witnessed with Mitzy, *that* had truly amazed her. His gentle bedside manner, his kindness and caring showed another side of his personality she'd never seen before. The memory left her fascinated.

Now they'd be working together, how had he phrased it? *Very closely.* The thought of it made her feel breathless, confused. For the sake of the bears and the patients who needed them, she'd have to get over that feeling. For the children, she could learn to deal with Dr. Kayne Frost in a calm, rational manner. She'd have to.

"Doc Berne?"

Taylor blinked at the concerned face of Flora Mills, Frost's eighty-year-old, chocolate-loving surgical patient. Flora, who had wheeled herself into the store during Taylor's reverie, clutched an ailing Teddy bear in her lap. Or what was left of one.

"Flora!" Taylor scolded softly. "What are you

doing out of bed so soon? Dr. Frost won't be pleased at all.''

Flora scowled. ''Ridiculous! I'm as fit as ever. But that's more than I can say for this bear of mine. Do you think you can patch him up, Doc?''

Taylor took the pitiful creature from Flora's protective grasp and made a precise assessment of the damage. Teddy had a three-inch wound in his side and a gaping tear in one felt paw. Stuffing was leaking from both holes. ''I think so,'' Taylor assured Flora, conscious of the woman's deep concern. ''He's tough, this one, built to last.''

Flora watched with trepidation, squinting sharply as Taylor explored the extent of his injuries. ''I had my son bring him down from the attic, after I saw your bear hospital. But, my word,'' she gasped, her quick eyes widening with morbid fascination. ''That's a nasty gash in his side. Do you suppose the dog got him?''

Taylor took another look at the bear. No, those injuries weren't inflicted by a dog. Dog attacks were more thorough. By the time she saw the victim, there was usually very little left. Small clumps of hair—the tattered remnant of an ear.

''It's hard to tell,'' she admitted in frustration. ''He may have been mauled by carpet beetles.''

Flora clutched the arm of her wheelchair. ''Oh, the poor thing!'' she whispered in horror.

Taylor nodded with enthusiasm. ''Or possibly . . . moths.''

Flora turned up the volume on her hearing aid. ''Moths?''

Taylor rubbed her chin. "Still, the fur's in marvelous condition. Long and curly. Except for that one patch on his stomach. Could be—" she paused, thinking.

Flora waited in silent agony, her expression grim.

"Dry rot!" Taylor pronounced.

Flora groaned and shook her head in agitation. "Doc, he's just like one of the family, is there anything you can do?"

Taylor smiled with the confidence of experience. "A routine operation, Mrs. Mills. And completely painless. Teddy won't feel a thing."

Flora sighed, greatly relieved. "Thank goodness. For a minute there, I was afraid he wouldn't pull through!"

Taylor carefully wrapped the bear in tissue paper. "Leave him with me, Mrs. Mills. By the time you're well, I'll make sure that Teddy is too. Then you can go home together."

Flora placed one shaky hand on Taylor's arm. "Thanks, Doc, I feel better already."

Taylor patted the woman's hand. A great-grandmother of eight, Mrs. Mills was a lot like her Teddy bear—worn out by too much love. But thanks to the skill of Dr. Kayne Frost, Flora had more time to share that love.

Flora drew her hand away and pointed to the tall figure approaching down the hall. "Here comes Dr. Frost now."

The old woman looked happy to see him. She showed not an ounce of remorse for being caught out of bed against doctor's orders. Dr. Frost, it seemed, did not strike fear in the hearts of his patients. Taylor wished she could feel the same way, but the glowering expression on his face inspired little confidence.

Frost stopped momentarily in the hall, speaking briefly to a uniformed nurse. Seconds later, the nurse walked directly into the gift shop and wheeled Flora away. Flora took it in stride, waving merrily to Dr. Frost as they passed in the hall.

When Frost continued in the direction of the shop, Taylor looked around for a hole to crawl into, knowing she would somehow be blamed for Flora's escape.

She didn't look up when he entered.

"Good afternoon, Miss Berne."

She saw the outline of long, lean legs under sharply pressed pants. She followed the well-muscled form up and up, gradually raising her head until she met his eyes. They were smiling.

Confused, Taylor frowned. "Dr. Frost, I—"

He shook his head. "Do us both a favor, Taylor Berne, don't explain."

She spread her hands out, palms up. "I don't understand."

Frost shrugged his shoulders in mock resignation. "You were about to explain why Flora Mills was here with you, when she had express orders to stay in bed."

Taylor nodded slowly.

Frost continued, his expression a study in patience. "She's now back in her room, resting comfortably. An explanation would only complicate matters further. And remember, I don't like complications."

How could she forget? But at least this time, he didn't intend to blame her unfairly. Taylor folded her arms across her chest. "Very well, Dr. Frost, if you didn't come in here for an explanation, why did you come?"

Unconsciously, he raised a hand to his face. "Shaving cream."

Taylor studied his face involuntarily, staring with interest at the faint shadow covering his chin and cheeks. "Shaving cream?" she repeated absently.

Frost inclined his head. "Precisely. Do you have any?"

"You didn't shave this morning?" she asked, curiosity winning over better judgement.

Frost cocked his head, raising his left eyebrow a fraction. "Do you always ask your customers such probing questions?"

Taylor's cheeks grew warm. "Sorry, just curious."

Frost's mouth twisted into a wry smile. "If you must know, I got called in very early this morning. Now that I have a few free minutes to shave, I've discovered I'm out of shaving cream."

Taylor continued staring. She couldn't keep her eyes off the dark, fascinating stubble on his chin. What would it feel like, she wondered, to run her fingers over that hard, scratchy surface? She lost herself in the thought, trying to imagine his rough, rugged skin moving against the soft surface of her cheek.

Frost grew impatient. "Well, do you have any?"

"Oh!" she jumped, forcing her eyes away from his face. What was she thinking? "Let me check."

Shaving cream, she muttered silently. It had to be around here somewhere. Taylor turned in the small space behind the counter. "Let me see." Her eyes searched the shelves high and low. She dug under the counter in an old cardboard box. "Not in there." She closed her eyes briefly. "Just give me a minute to think."

Frost drummed his fingers on the counter. "Miss Berne. . . . "

"I know we have some, Dr. Frost. I'm sure of it." She cleared aside some dusty bottles from the lower shelf.

"Hairspray, mouthwash, tissues, peanuts—" she paused. "Peanuts! I wonder where those came from?"

Dr. Frost, his jaw set in a hard line, attempted a smile. "I'm sure I don't know."

Taylor flipped the jar aside. "Oh well, let's see what else we have back here." She continued the search.

"Miss Berne," Frost growled.

Taylor stopped, riveted by the tone of his voice. "Yes?"

"I'm in a hurry," he breathed with pained tolerance.

She nodded. "I understand completely. Maybe you'd like to stop by later?" She gave him a proud smile. "We don't just carry bears in here, we also stock all the basic necessities."

His eyes widened in incredulity as he gave her a look reserved for the hopelessly insane. "Never mind," he told her. "I'll use soap."

Taylor shrugged and made a futile attempt to arrange the jumbled shelves into some order.

Frost's tone grew serious. "Tomorrow morning, I'd like you to visit a few patients with me."

She looked up, hesitant. ''So soon?''

Frost nodded. ''The sooner we start compiling data, the more information I'll have to present to the hospital board.''

And the longer she'd have to convince Frost to support her program. Doc Berne would not let her patients down.

She gave him a level stare. ''I'll be ready.''

But would she ever be ready to confront the sheer force of Dr. Kayne Frost? No, she whispered softly to herself. Never.

Chapter 3

"And don't bring that cart!"

Taylor frowned, remembering Dr. Frost's warning words. How did he expect her to bring the bears along on this morning's rounds if she didn't bring the cart? Okay, so maybe it got in the way before, but was that enough reason to make her leave it behind?

No, she thought dejectedly, it wasn't. But she wouldn't argue the point. Not when she needed to win Frost over to her side. She would handle him in a more diplomatic way from now on.

Didn't Nita always say you could catch more flies with honey than vinegar? Or maybe she meant bears. Yes, you could definitely catch more bears with honey.

But Dr. Frost was no Teddy bear. With his dark hair and menacing eyes, he was more the grizzly type. The image of power and strength—of animal force held closely in check. Too closely.

According to folklore, the bear stood for passion as a force of nature. But Dr. Frost was not a passionate man. Or was he?

What else could you call a man who gave every bit

45

of himself to his work? What better way to win him to her cause than by working together?

Then Frost would surely see that although their methods were different, their goals were the same—to provide the best possible patient care. That was the operative word—*care*. She'd have to remember that word to get through the morning with Dr. Frost. She'd have to be diplomatic.

So, in this new spirit of diplomacy, Taylor left her cart stored safely in the closet. She slipped on her multipocketed lavender jacket and scouted the store's shelves and crannies, gathering small bears here and there to take with her. If Frost didn't want the cart, she'd simply bring some smaller bears along for a ride.

She stuffed one in the lapel pocket, two more in the pockets at her waist, another in the hidden lining pocket. The last gave her an odd little bulge at the stomach, but it was hardly noticeable. Overall, the effect was unobtrusive. Now she was properly armed to face Mitzy Pearl and the rest of Frost's patients.

It wasn't so easy to face Dr. Frost himself. He paced impatiently outside the gift shop door, eager for them to be on their way. When Taylor met him in the hall, he surveyed her briefly. If he objected to the traveling bears, whose heads peeked silently from the openings of her jacket, he made no comment.

He uttered a crisp good morning, then launched into a brief rundown of the patients they would be visiting. Mitzy was first on the list. Taylor sighed inwardly. Well, nobody had said it was going to be easy.

"About the Pearl case," Frost said as they made their way to her room. "Don't give her any bears."

Taylor's voice rose in surprise. "Then what am I here for?"

Frost eyed her sternly. "What *you're* here for is still open for debate. *I'm* here to provide good medical care. I can't do that without the support of the hospital staff. That includes you, Miss Berne. When I give a direct medical order, I expect it to be obeyed."

Taylor stopped dead in her tracks and folded her arms across her chest. "How do you expect me to demonstrate the beneficial effects of the bears if I can't give them to your patients?"

Frost reached out to cup her chin in his hand, turning her face toward him. "Contrary to what you may believe, I'm not a complete ogre. Personally, I wouldn't mind if that little girl had a dozen bears, but medically, it's not advisable."

The warm electricity of his touch made her stomach tingle with a strange excitement. She looked away, confused. "Why not?"

Frost released her, dropping both hands in the pockets of his lab coat. "A heart condition is just one of Mitzy's problems. She's also highly allergic. She's forbidden contact with anything that could irritate her respiratory tract. That includes the bacteria, molds, and yeast that may be present on your Teddy bears."

Taylor searched his face with growing dismay. "You mean she's never had a stuffed animal of any kind?"

Frost's jaw tightened perceptibly, as if he too found the situation disturbing. "Too risky."

Taylor's heart lurched. Mitzy was very sick, with

no soft hugs to comfort her, no Teddy bears to turn to. No wonder she'd become a difficult child.

"But what can I do to help?" Taylor asked, wondering how to console Mitzy without the aid of any bears.

Frost shrugged, and dug his hands deeper into his pockets. "I'm not sure. But this is one patient who could use some of that 'magic' you're supposed to have."

Taylor's spirits sank. Had Frost done this on purpose, shown her the most difficult case first, the one where she was sure to fail? Was he purposely trying to discourage her? Or was he genuinely concerned for Mitzy, hoping that the attention would have some positive effect on the girl?

"Remember," he told her when they reached Mitzy's room, "no physical contact with the bears. No touching or holding. Just looking."

When they entered her room, Mitzy was wide awake, propped up in bed with her frail arms folded primly in her lap.

"Where's my breakfast?" she demanded with a practiced composure far too advanced for her years.

Frost laughed, his aqua eyes sparkling like the morning sun on a mountain lake. He took Mitzy's defiance in stride, completely unfazed by her petulant behavior. "Coming right up, Your Highness. In the meantime, I've brought you a visitor." He turned to Taylor and gave her a broad wink. "Doc Berne, meet your new patient."

If only he hadn't winked at her that way. The wink

took Taylor by surprise. She stammered. "Mitzy . . . pleas—pleased to meet you."

The perceptive child sensed her weakness immediately. She narrowed her eyes and regarded Taylor with deep suspicion. "Go 'way," she told Taylor. "Don't want another doctor. I've got Doctor Frost."

Taylor bit her lip, feeling her composure slip farther away. Nothing like making a good first impression. Well, it couldn't get any worse.

She gave Mitzy a tentative smile. "I'm not replacing Dr. Frost," she assured the glaring child. "In fact, I'm not really a doctor at all."

Mitzy stuck out her tongue. "Go *away*."

Wonderful, Taylor sighed inwardly. Just wonderful. Frost was probably enjoying every minute of this. She stole a glance in his direction.

He folded his arms across his chest and leaned against the wall, an amused smile on his face. His expression clearly read—"Go ahead, let's see what you can do now."

Taylor turned her attention back to Mitzy, studying the child with growing trepidation. Most of the patients were glad to have visitors of any sort. Mitzy wanted to throw her out of the room.

Taylor resisted the impulse to follow the child's orders. She wouldn't give up that easily, especially not in front of Dr. Frost.

She reached inside one pocket and withdrew a teacup-sized Teddy. She held him up for Mitzy to see, then spoke in a low, soothing voice. "Mr. Bear says *please* don't send me away."

Mitzy gave Taylor a very adult scowl, picked up the

plastic water glass on her nightstand and hurled it into the air.

Dr. Frost stood directly in the path of the flying glass, but luckily his reflexes were very fast. He ducked.

Mr. Bear was not so lucky. The glass bounced off the wall and hit him soundly, knocking him out of Taylor's palm. He hit the floor with a pitiful thud and a hurt, high-pitched squeak.

Shocked by Mitzy's extreme behavior, Taylor bent to retrieve Mr. Bear. She had every intention of giving the child a strong lecture on bad manners.

But it wasn't necessary. Mitzy knew she'd gone too far. Her bright blue eyes filled with tears and one tiny hand flew to her mouth. "Did I hurt him?" she cried.

Mr. Bear had come to no harm, but Taylor knew an opportunity from heaven when she saw one. She made a great pretense of examining Mr. Bear for possible injuries, checking his scruffy limbs with painstaking care. Perhaps Mitzy could learn by example.

"He seems to be okay," she finally told the worried child. "Nothing's broken."

Mitzy sniffed, wringing her dainty hands together. "I'm sorry I hit your bear. I wish I could hold him."

Taylor bit her lip, overwhelmed by an acute yearning to help the child. But there was nothing she could do. So much for her 'magic' Teddy bears.

She sent Frost a look of helpless appeal.

Sensing her desperation, he stepped smoothly into the conversation. "Tell you what," he said to Mitzy, "you let me listen to your heart with this stethoscope and then I'll let you listen to mine. Deal?"

Mitzy's eyes glimmered with interest. "Really?"

Frost gave her a serious nod. "Really."

Mitzy puffed up her chest. "Okay. Deal."

The examination proceeded calmly from that point, thanks to Frost's easy bedside manner. Taylor couldn't help admiring his relaxed attitude toward this hard-to-handle patient. He looked as carefree as a loving father playing Sunday morning games with his daughter.

Taylor stopped herself before she could follow that train of thought to its logical conclusion. She'd been about to admit that Kayne Frost would make a good father. The very idea was ridiculous. She knew, better than anyone, that overworked doctors did *not* make good fathers.

She turned away from the cozy scene and waited for Frost in the hall. Her stomach churned wretchedly. So far, she was off to a dreadful start. She hadn't done much to help Mitzy. Of course, Frost would make a note of her failure in his meticulous medical log.

But when he joined her outside Mitzy's door, Frost simply smiled encouragingly. A smile? She could hardly believe it, especially after her miserable performance with Mitzy. Was there a milliliter of compassion mixed with the ice in his veins?

They visited several more surgical candidates, and Taylor's bears were met with more typical delighted responses. The last patient on the list was a young boy, obviously terrified over the prospect of his impending heart operation.

"Dr. Frost," the boy whispered, his bright hair and freckles in sharp contrast to his pale face, "will it hurt much?"

Frost sat on the edge of the boy's bed. "Well, let

me think. You'll be asleep for the operation, so *that* certainly won't hurt. When you wake up it's going to hurt some, but not for very long. Besides, you'll have something to show for your bravery—a fine scar.''

''A scar!'' the boy exclaimed. ''Like a pirate's?''

Frost nodded, and a wave of dark hair fell across his forehead. ''Exactly.''

The boy's eyes lit up as all traces of fear vanished. ''Show me, Dr. Frost. Show me where my scar will be.''

Frost turned to Taylor, smiling. ''Dr. Berne,'' he said, his aqua eyes twinkling, ''I wonder if you would assist me with a minor operation?''

She would do anything if he continued to look at her that way. ''Yes?''

He eyed her jacket. ''Have you got a spare Teddy bear in one of those lumpy pockets?''

Surprised, Taylor nodded. What was he up to now? She searched briefly, then handed Frost a new, brown plush bear. ''Right here.''

He took it, nodding with approval. ''I think he'll do just fine. Wait here, please.''

Frost disappeared for a few minutes, returning with a surgical razor. He turned to the boy. ''Now watch carefully.''

Frost proceeded to shave the little bear's chest area, working with clean, precise strokes. A wispy mound of fur fell to the floor. He set aside the razor, took a red felt marker from his jacket, and proceeded to draw a simple red heart on the Teddy's exposed chest.

''This,'' he explained as he worked, ''is where your scar will be. From here,'' he pointed to an area just above the heart, "to here," he said, drawing some red ink 'stitches' on the bear's abdomen.

The boy watched the procedure, fascinated, then looked up at Frost with open admiration. "Wow," he breathed. "Pretty neat."

Frost handed him the bear. "You can keep him," Frost suggested, "for further examination."

"Thanks!"

Taylor fought back a lump in her throat, unexpectedly moved by Frost's patience and understanding. He had turned the boy's fear into excitement. She wanted to compliment him, to say something that acknowledged his kindness.

For a moment, when he turned to her, Taylor felt something pass between them, a warm look in his eyes that mirrored the empathy in her own. But a second later it was gone, replaced by the cool demeanor of Kayne Frost, the clinical cardiac surgeon.

"We'd better get out of here," he told her. "I'm late for surgery."

Taylor swept the gift-shop floor at the end of another long day. Over the past week, she'd spent several early mornings with Dr. Frost, handing out bears and lending support wherever needed. Surprisingly, the arrangement was working out fairly well. Together, they seemed to have been able to help many patients.

Frost hadn't discussed the results with her, presumably reserving his judgment for presentation to the hospital board in five weeks. By then, Taylor hoped to convince him that her bear therapy held more advantages for the patients than disadvantages. If she could stay out of trouble for that long and not create any further "disasters", her prospects for success looked good.

Taylor made her final preparations to leave for the evening. She returned the broom to the storage closet, secured the cash register and reached over to switch off the dancing clock-radio bear. But the cumulative effects of the week left her tired and clumsy—she accidentally knocked the bear to the floor. His furry limbs continued wiggling to the mood of the music.

"I'm sorry, Moe," she apologized to his homely, forgiving face. "I guess this week's been harder than I realized."

Taylor returned him to his position on the counter and switched his button to turn off the music. Moe's dancing slowed, then finally stopped altogether. She let herself out of the shop and made her way home.

During the short drive to her apartment, Taylor barely noticed the sultry beauty of the tropical winter evening. Nighthawks skimmed the sky for insects on the wing. Gardenia blossoms perfumed the air, their fragrance as rich as ancient incense, and a few poinsettias had flowered, their red foliage ready to welcome in the holiday season. A cool breeze blew in from the ocean, but it wasn't enough to blow the worry from Taylor's mind.

She couldn't stop thinking about little Mitzy Pearl. Mitzy was the one child she had been unable to help, the one sad case she couldn't forget. Despite Taylor's repeated efforts, the little girl remained stubborn and belligerent. Surely, there must be a way to comfort the lonely child.

It was hard to imagine that Mitzy had never cuddled a stuffed animal to her chest, never had a soft, furry toy to love. No wonder the child acted the way she did. Taylor wanted to do *something* to help. But what?

As soon as she opened the front door of her cozy two-room apartment, Taylor felt a light tap-tapping against her shin. She smiled and bent to scoop her darling Patches into her arms. A mixed-up medley of assorted and unbecoming colors, Patches was definitely in the running for world's ugliest cat. But Taylor loved him anyway.

When she'd first seen him at the local animal shelter, Patches had already spent three hopeful weeks waiting to be adopted. A sucker for any hard-luck case, Taylor made the fateful mistake of petting him through the wire cage. Patches knew an easy target when he saw one. He turned his purring machine up to full blast and gave her his most pathetic stare. The matter was settled. She *had* to adopt him. No one else would.

Patches was so grateful to be rescued that he rewarded her with a sweet, soothing disposition, purring at any opportunity, and regarded her with an affection that might've made his fancier, more sophisticated feline relatives contemptuous. Tonight, with an empty belly and a furry neck just waiting to be rubbed, Patches was as happy to see her as ever.

"I suppose you want your dinner," she speculated, as Patches leapt from her arms and led her hopefully into the tiny kitchen. "Don't worry, old boy. I know the routine by now. Cat food is always the first priority. *Then* mommy can have her own dinner."

Patches' ears perked up at the sound of the can

opener. When Taylor put the food in front of him, he attacked the meal with a very un-catlike enthusiasm. Taylor ruffled the fur on his head. "Patches," she sighed. "You're not a very exemplary cat. Couldn't you at least *try* to act finicky?"

Patches didn't seem to hear. He polished off every scrap of food on his plate, then settled back to clean his face and paws fastidiously and with great satisfaction.

With Patches taken care of, Taylor heated a plate of leftover spaghetti and ate it in front of her small television. But the evening news turned out to be exceptionally depressing, so she turned it off and stretched out on her second-hand couch to read magazines. Anything to take her mind off work.

But the magazines sparked her subconscious and an idea struck her suddenly, an obscure memory of an article she'd read in *Teddy Collector*. She thumbed through the stack on her polished oak coffee table, searching for the particular past-issue she needed. With any luck, that article would contain the answer to Mitzy's problem.

Taylor couldn't resist reading a bit along the way, an ad here, an editorial there, and as the hours ticked by, she lost herself in many interesting articles. It was nearly midnight when she finally found the right one, a piece written by the mother of an allergy-prone child. Just as Taylor finished reading, the phone rang. She slipped the magazine into her purse, deciding to show it to Dr. Frost in the morning.

She picked up the phone. "Hello?"

"Miss Berne?"

The sound of the cool, authoritative voice made her sit up straight. "Dr. Frost?"

His tone simmered with irritation. "It's a good thing you're there."

Taylor frowned, glancing at her watch. Why was Dr. Frost calling her at this hour? And why did he sound so angry?

"Dr. Frost," she said, "I can barely hear you. Can you speak a little louder?"

In the background she heard loud rock-and-roll music. Was Dr. Frost at a party? She could've sworn it was his night to be on call. Besides, he was hardly the partying type.

His voice grew louder as the background noise increased. "Sorry to disturb you, Miss Berne, but I'm in the middle of a disturbance myself."

Taylor held the earpiece at a more comfortable distance. Really, whatever it was, he didn't have to shout *that* loud. "Would you mind turning down that music?" she asked firmly.

Frost raised his voice to an alarming pitch. "I'd love to. In fact, there's nothing I'd love more. But I can't. That *music*, if you can call it that, is right next door to the pay phone I'm calling from. It's coming from your gift shop."

Taylor gripped the phone tighter, drawing it closer to her ear. "What did you say?"

Frost's voice took on an unnatural tremor, the usual even tone replaced by a quavering shout. "I said it's coming from your gift shop! Get back to the hospital, Miss Berne. Now! And bring the key!"

He hung up the phone, making Taylor jump at the

ominous click. For a full minute, she simply stared at the receiver. Music coming from the gift shop? She couldn't explain it. But one thing was certain, she'd better get back to the hospital. And quick.

She grabbed her purse and raced out the door.

At the hospital, the scene was worse than she'd imagined. The usual nighttime peace was shattered by a screeching din emanating from the shop. Harried orderlies scurried back and forth down the halls, and the nurse in charge of the patient call station threw up her hands in despair.

In the midst of the confusion, Kayne Frost paced outside the gift shop door, his arms folded across his chest in silent resignation.

Well, Taylor thought with rising hope, at least Dr. Frost had calmed himself since their phone conversation. But when she saw the expression on his face, the glimmer of hope flickered and died. Dr. Frost, calm? She'd never seen him so angry.

The rock-and-roll music crashed around them, hot and loud. The male vocalist lamented to the unrelenting beat in a feverish frenzy. "Got to have you baaaaaby . . ."

Frost's eyes flashed with cold, blue fire. "Turn it off, Miss Berne," he ordered between clenched teeth.

Taylor fumbled in her handbag, searching for the key. "What is it, Dr. Frost? What's making that terrible racket?"

"Ohhh, baaaby . . ."

Frost pressed his finger against the glass door of the gift shop, pointing directly at Moe. "*That's* what's making the noise. It's that blasted bear. It's a radio or something.''

Taylor blinked at the sight of her dancing clock-radio bear. His small, furry body gyrated wildly to the boot-stomping beat. ''Got to have yooou . . . ''

Taylor's mouth formed a silent O. Something must have malfunctioned in Moe's internal mechanism. She was sure she'd turned him off.

''Miss Berne,'' Frost warned, his voice a hoarse whisper. ''If you don't locate those keys in the next ten seconds, I will personally break this door in and silence that miserable creature forever.''

Taylor dug deeper in her bag, then, noting Frost's stormy look, abandoned all sense of decorum and dumped the contents of her purse onto the floor. She grabbed for the keys. ''Here they are!''

With lightning speed she turned the key in the lock, threw back the dead-bolt and raced for Moe. She reached the button before he made yet another pelvic thrust. ''Ohhh Baaa—''

Abruptly, a peaceful silence reigned as Taylor slumped against the counter.

Frost followed her inside and sank into a nearby chair. His sigh of relief hung in the air between them, louder somehow in the sudden quiet than the rock-and-roll had been.

''How?'' he breathed in disbelief. ''How did this happen?''

Taylor shook her head. ''I don't understand it. I turned him off before I left, I'm sure of it. Unless . . . ''

Frost narrowed his eyes. ''Yes?''

Taylor bent to inspect Moe. ''Well, I did drop him

earlier. I wonder if—oh.'' She stopped. ''So that's what happened.''

He folded his arms across his chest. ''Don't keep me in suspense.''

Taylor eyed him doubtfully. Dr. Frost was in no condition to hear her unfortunate explanation. She proceeded cautiously. ''His alarm switch was turned to **ON**. I must have switched it to the wrong position by mistake, after I dropped him. The alarm was set for twelve-twenty and when it went off, well, the volume goes up automatically—''

She stopped. Something in Frost's expression kept her from explaining further. His mouth started twitching with uncontrolled amusement. His face broke into a smile. Then he threw back his head and filled the room with rich, full-bodied laughter.

Taylor's jaw dropped open as she watched him in astonishment. Dr. Frost laughing? No one would believe it. She could hardly believe it herself. She thought of the bear wiggling his hips while Frost stood helplessly outside the door watching. Frost's wonderful laugh was contagious, and she suddenly found herself laughing right along with him.

The night nurse found them like that, doubled over with hilarity, tears of mirth streaming down their cheeks.

''Dr. Frost?'' she asked suspiciously. ''Is that you?''

Frost attempted a measure of control. ''It's me, Miss Morgan. Everything's back to normal. Tell everyone the emergency's over.''

The nurse looked doubtfully from Dr. Frost to Taylor and back again, but she didn't ask any more questions.

She left in a great hurry, apparently convinced that Dr. Frost had lapsed into a state of hysteria.

Frost looked at Taylor. "Come on. Let's get out of here before my somber reputation is completely in shreds." He gave her a wry smile. "We wouldn't want to give anyone the idea that I'm *human* after all, now would we?"

Without waiting for a response, Frost took her by the arm. He stopped while she gathered up the contents of her purse, then led her deftly to a quiet booth in the hospital cafeteria. The room was nearly deserted.

Frost poured coffee for both of them and sat staring at her over the rim of his cup. "What am I going to do with you, Miss Berne? This hospital will never be normal with you around." He smiled warmly. "Neither will I."

Taylor's heart did a flip-flop in her chest. Sitting across a cozy booth from Kayne Frost made her feel anything but normal. His very proximity sent her emotions spinning. She gave him a tentative smile, her tawny eyes bright with mischief. "Maybe this place could use a little shaking up."

Frost grinned. "I think you've done that already. You're about as subtle as an earthquake."

Taylor started laughing again. "You seem pretty shock-proof to me."

Frost shook his head. "Not so. You continue to torment me, even though I've made every attempt to avoid you and that mixed-up menagerie of yours. It hasn't worked."

Taylor took a sip of her coffee. Avoiding Frost hadn't worked for her either. If he wasn't around in person, his image was always there, lurking at the back of her mind, compelling, forbidding.

Frost gave her a speculative stare. "Maybe I need to change my tactics—get to know the enemy better—embrace the danger. What do you think?"

She thought his eyes were the most fascinating shade of blue she'd ever seen. Twin pools of warm aquamarine water.

He continued, not waiting for an answer. "I think we can start by dropping the formalities, changing to first names. Agreed?"

She nodded. "If you say so, Dr. Frost."

He laughed. "No, my name's Kayne. Will you call me that, Taylor?"

The sound of her name rolling off his tongue was smooth, melodious. She let it float around her. "All right . . . Kayne."

He nodded with satisfaction. "That's better. Now maybe you can tell me a little more about yourself, like why those Teddy bears are so important to you."

Taylor could barely contain her surprise. Dr. Frost, no, Kayne, actually seemed interested. And oddly enough, she felt the desire to share her feelings with him.

She glanced down at her coffee mug, suddenly shy. "I was asthmatic for most of my childhood," she explained quietly. "I outgrew it eventually, but all that time spent in the hospital was pretty scary."

She shrugged, looking up to meet his eyes. "I know there are plenty of kids who've been through worse, but children don't always know the difference between one medical problem and the next. They only know when they're scared and lonely.''

Frost exhaled softly. ''What about your parents? Didn't they come to visit you?''

Taylor shook her head. ''My mom died when I was seven, and my dad was a very busy man.'' She gave him a knowing smile. ''A doctor. Like you.''

Kayne raised his eyebrows. ''A surgeon?''

She gripped the rim of her cup. ''No, but very dedicated. And just as busy.''

He looked away. ''The family always pays the price.''

She nodded, touched by his understanding, and continued. ''My mother gave me a Teddy bear before she died, a family heirloom that originally belonged to my grandmother. He was a fine, early bear, made by a famous German toymaker. He's quite valuable now, the kind of vintage rarity highly sought after by collectors. You may remember him, the big honey-colored fellow named Mr. Marmalade.''

Kayne nodded hesitantly. ''Is he the one with the crooked ears?''

Taylor smiled. ''I like to think of them as artistically placed. Anyway, that bear went with me on every hospital visit. He was a sort of security blanket, only better.'' She laughed, warm humor glowing in her eyes. ''Anyone can tell how much I loved him. His nose is nearly kissed away!''

Kayne studied her face, his eyes settling on her lips. ''An interesting prospect,'' he murmured.

Taylor felt a warm blush steal across her cheeks. She hurried to finish her story. ''He's been with me ever since. When I took this job as gift shop manager, I realized it was my chance to share a little of that comfort with the patients who need it.''

He studied her face. ''You do have a remarkable effect on children. Does that come from personal experience? I noticed you had several young admirers with you at lunch the other day.''

She smiled. ''Those three belong to a friend of mine. I just play substitute aunt every once in a while.''

His eyes flashed with amusement. ''And administer ice cream as needed?''

Taylor flushed, remembering the silly, sticky picture she must have made. ''They love chocolate.''

''So I observed,'' he commented drily. ''And you, Taylor, what do you love? Besides Teddy bears and children and vanilla cream?''

She looked down at her coffee and shrugged. ''I love my work.''

He nodded and reached out across the table to touch her hand. ''Well, that's one thing we have in common.''

She looked up at him. ''But I don't believe work should be the most important thing in a person's life.''

He laced his fingers idly through hers. ''Sometimes, it just takes over until there isn't room for anything else.''

Take a hint, Taylor, she told herself sternly. You're the *thing* there isn't any room for.

She pulled her hand away. ''That reminds me!'' she said as brightly as she could manage. ''I think I've figured out a way to help Mitzy Pearl.''

Frost smiled at her enthusiasm. ''Oh?''

"I remembered reading an article about it." She pulled the *Teddy Collector* from her purse and thumbed the glossy pages. "Yes, here it is," she held the article up for Kayne to see. "Look—non-allergenic bears!"

He leaned over the table with growing interest. "Microbiologically efficient?"

Taylor suppressed a smile. "Exactly. The bears are prepared in packaging to eliminate any harmful spores, and presto! Perfect for squeezing instead of wheezing or sneezing."

Kayne nodded thoughtfully, "This should work." He studied her closely, his eyes locked with hers for one breathless moment. "Good job."

Taylor's heart swelled with a sudden surge of pride. "I'll order the bear right away. I can't wait to see the look on Mitzy's face."

Kayne continued to watch her. "I hope it's like the look on yours."

Taylor looked away, flustered. What was wrong with her? The man paid her a simple compliment, and she went completely to pieces. She hardly recognized herself. She hardly recognized *him*.

Her image of Dr. Frost as the operating robot no longer seemed accurate. This was a man who cared, perhaps a little too much, about medicine. No, about patients.

Taylor felt a pang of envy, so sharp and hot that it almost made her wince. With a certain amount of shame, she had to admit that she was jealous of those patients. She had to admit she wanted Kayne to care about *her*.

But that was impossible. He had no time for relationships, certainly not with a bumbling bear doctor. And besides, she had no room for further heartache.

She would have to be very careful over the next five weeks. Working with Kayne was going to be more difficult than she had realized, difficult in ways she never imagined.

Dr. Frost was very good at healing hearts, but something inside told her he could break them just as easily. And Taylor intended to keep hers in one piece.

Chapter 4

"He's really mine?" Mitzy asked, her china-blue eyes brimming with tears. "And I can really hold him?"

Taylor nodded, a lump in her throat as she handed Mitzy the clear, plastic container with the non-allergenic bear sealed inside. "He's all yours," she assured the child. "I'm sure you two will be friends forever."

Mitzy's trembling hands closed around the see-through cylinder, holding her new Teddy as if he might try to escape. She pressed her nose against the plastic, kissing him through the package. "I love you," she whispered, cuddling the container close to her chest.

Kayne, who stood on the other side of Mitzy's bed, grinned at Taylor. He knelt by the bed and addressed Mitzy solemnly. "You can keep the bear, Mitzy, but only if I can keep the package."

Mitzy held the bear closer. "You mean, you want me to let him *out*?"

Kayne nodded, his eyes dancing like a blue-morning mist on the ocean. "This time, it's all right."

Mitzy gave Kayne a disbelieving stare and turned to

67

Taylor, checking to see if all the adults had gone crazy or if it was just Dr. Frost who had lost his mind.

Taylor gestured to the package. ''Go ahead, honey. Open it.''

Mitzy didn't wait long enough for the ''doctors'' to change their minds. She fumbled with the seal, broke it open, and lifted the bear gently from his plastic home. ''Ohhh,'' she sighed, petting her new Teddy on his shaggy head. ''He's soooo soft!''

Taylor smiled, blinking back the tears. Mitzy's expression was her reward, reflecting the warm glow in her own heart. She'd ordered the bear by express mail, and it had arrived only two days later. This moment of joy made the extra effort worthwhile. This was magic.

She tore her gaze away from Mitzy's face to study Kayne's reaction. The look in his eyes told her how much the scene had touched him, too. He met her glance with one of deep understanding, a naked, open stare more intimate than a lover's caress.

Flustered by the intensity of his gaze, Taylor turned back to Mitzy. ''Maybe,'' she told the child weakly, her heart racing, ''I'll be able to stop by to see you and Teddy later. In the meantime, I'm sure you'd like to get better acquainted with your bear, maybe pick a name for him?''

Mitzy nodded, a cherubic smile on her face. Even if it was only temporary, the bear had already worked a minor miracle. Mitzy was calm and cooperative.

Taylor turned to go.

Kayne stopped her at the foot of the bed, placing his hand on her shoulder. ''Just a moment, please.''

She glanced down involuntarily, compelled to study the angry, dark scar drawn across the golden tan of his wrist and knuckles. She fought the inexplicable urge to reach out and trace her fingers across the jagged edges.

She turned to face him, regaining her composure. "Is there something else you need, Dr. Frost?"

In front of the patients, Taylor continued to address him formally, thinking that it sounded more professional. But there were other reasons for her propriety, reasons that had nothing to do with the patients.

She clung to the title more to remind *herself*, not the patients, that this was Dr. Frost, the clinical, cardiac surgeon. She forced herself to keep the barrier between them, to emphasize that this was Frost the doctor. Ever since the evening in the cafeteria, she'd been unable to forget that he was Kayne the man.

He brought her back to reality, his hand on her shoulder propelling her into the hall. "Yes," he replied, "there is something else. I'd like a moment to speak with you."

She studied his eyes for a clue of the tension reflected in his voice. "What is it?" she asked, a shiver of apprehension snaking down her spine.

Kayne ran his fingers roughly through his hair. "I didn't want to tell you before, not until I knew for sure." He gave her a speculative glance. "I was afraid you'd worry unnecessarily."

Taylor swallowed uneasily, wondering what sort of news the usually matter-of-fact Kayne could want to protect her from. "Worry about what?"

"Mitzy," he said, his voice solemn. "I've already discussed it with her parents."

Taylor's heart sank. "Kayne," she murmured, tugging at his sleeve, "Mitzy's not in danger. . . . " Her voice trailed away at the look in his eyes.

"Not if I can help it," he answered vehemently.

He turned away, raking a dark wave of hair from his forehead. "This is always the hardest part," he muttered, "telling the family and friends. Even the surgery's easier than this."

Taylor took a deep breath. "Please," she said quietly. "I can handle it. She's not getting any better, is she?"

Kayne shook his head. "Not by herself. She needs another test, a heart catheterization, to check the pressure gradients in her heart."

Taylor winced. "Is it serious?"

"Any invasive heart procedure is serious. But with a little luck she'll pull through it."

Luck. Taylor knew it had very little to do with luck and a lot to do with the skill of the surgeon. She studied his face. "Will you be doing the procedure?"

"I will," he assured her. "I'd do it tomorrow, but it's not an emergency, and the surgical team deserves to spend Thanksgiving day with their families. Friday should be fine."

Thanksgiving. She'd nearly forgotten the holiday with the recent adjustments in her schedule. Was Kayne's work ethic rubbing off on her, too? He'd probably stay at the hospital straight through Christmas if he could.

Reflexively, Taylor's eyes went to his hands—so

firm and hard, so skilled, so *powerful*. Just looking at those hands and knowing Kayne would be in charge gave Taylor great comfort. Even the scar on his right hand was a reassuring sight.

For months, the nurses had speculated about that scar. The jagged gash was in the shape of a lightning bolt, symbolizing the potent energy within the man. How had it happened? A car accident? A knife fight with a jealous husband? A quick wrestle with an angry alligator? The theories ranged from the reasonable to the ridiculous. However he had acquired it, Taylor saw it as a brand of honor, a mark of skill, a badge of ability.

"You look upset," he told her, the concern evident on his face. "Better sit down for a minute."

He led her to a deserted waiting lounge and into a nearby chair. "I know it's a bit of a shock. Mitzy seems to have become special to you."

She took another deep breath to steady herself. She'd expected Mitzy to recover quickly and return home as spunky as ever. She'd known the child had a heart condition, and had been admitted to the hospital for a battery of tests, but she'd never dreamed the child's disability would get any worse.

Stupidly, she'd imagined that getting Mitzy a bear would somehow solve the rest of the child's problems. Intellectually, she'd known it wasn't possible, but emotionally, she'd hoped for a miracle.

Kayne sank into a chair beside her, leaning back against the wall, briefly closing his eyes. "Don't make yourself crazy with worry," he said. "You've done your best for the child. Now it's my turn."

Taylor blinked in surprise. He'd guessed her thoughts exactly. He knew precisely how she felt about Mitzy. Could he also guess the way she felt about him? Blushing hotly, she gave him a doubtful glance.

While Kayne's eyes were still closed, Taylor took a moment to study his face, to observe the perfect, angular planes, the hard curves that forged together in bold, masculine beauty. His profile was strong, as if drawn by an artist with daring, defiant strokes, softened only by the luxuriant fringe of thick eyelashes and the smooth, sensual fullness of his lips.

But there were shadows in the fineness of his face. He looked tired, no, exhausted. He looked in need of a long nap, a home-cooked meal, the comfort of a family. *His* family.

Taylor jerked herself to attention. Kayne Frost did not *have* a family. He understood there was no way to include the demands of a family in his grueling schedule of work. He'd even told her in so many words: "The family always pays the price."

Still, the fine lines etched at the corners of his eyes, the darkening circles around the lids, these brought out her strongest feminine instincts. She clenched her fist into a tight ball to keep from reaching out to smooth the lines from his face, resisting the urge to comfort him with soft, soothing words.

She stood slowly. "I appreciate you telling me about this, Kayne. What time tomorrow is Mitzy's catheterization? I'd like to be close by."

He opened his eyes, rubbing the lids with the back of his hands, fighting back a weary yawn. "Ten A.M. I'll find you afterwards, to let you know how it went."

She nodded, grateful for his concern. "Thank you."

He gave her a tired grin. "It's the least I can do for a favored colleague."

Taylor returned his grin with a studied scowl. He was teasing her again, trying to lighten the mood with a reference to her unwitting "doctor" status. But instead of making her laugh, the appealing, boyish gleam in his eyes nearly took her breath away.

In self-preservation, she turned to go.

"Oh, Doc Berne," he called after her.

She didn't turn around, but simply stopped in her tracks. "Yes?"

"The bear was a big hit. I'm sure Mitzy will get a good night's sleep tonight."

"I hope so," she responded, and hurried down the hall.

If Kayne's prediction came true for Mitzy, it did not come true for Taylor. She barely slept a wink all night. She couldn't stop worrying about Mitzy. She couldn't stop worrying about Kayne and her own reaction to him.

There was nothing she could do for Mitzy but wait. As for Kayne, well, she wasn't exactly sure how she felt about him. She only knew she *did* feel about him. Very strongly.

Her attraction for Kayne was a lot like catching the flu. Whenever he was near, her body shivered, her insides felt queasy, and her mind turned to mush. Kayne Frost was a dangerous disease she couldn't seem to shake.

It was completely normal, she reassured herself. Her

feelings were stronger now because she and Kayne were working together. No woman could come in close contact with him, day after day, and not feel *something*. The Frost epidemic was definitely catching. She simply had a very bad case. Sooner or later, she promised herself, she would get over it. Thanksgiving day spent at Nita's house passed in a blur. The usual joy she felt was marred by the restless jumble of worries in her head.

Back home, she tumbled into bed, and her alarm went off seconds later—at least, it seemed that way. Exhausted, not quite ready to face the day ahead, she showered, applied the usual minimum of make-up and headed for the hospital.

She spent the morning pacing the gift shop floor, rearranging the shelves, agonizing over Mitzy. Flora Mills stopped by, completely recovered and as spry as ever. Flora's joyful reunion with her newly restored Teddy helped distract Taylor for a while, but as soon as the woman and her bear were gone, Taylor resumed her nervous pacing.

Concentrating on Kayne helped relieve her mind, thinking about his confidence, his experience, his skill. There was power in those hands, the power to save lives. Kayne would use that power today, right now, to perform the procedure on Mitzy.

The clock hands in Moe's stomach indicated the procedure would soon be over. Taylor couldn't stand it any longer. She hung the "back in twenty minutes" sign on the gift shop door and made her way to the operating room.

She didn't have long to wait. Kayne emerged shortly

and spoke to Mitzy's parents. From the relieved expression on their faces, Taylor could tell that everything was fine. The couple hugged each other, then turned to shake Kayne's hand. They left to go and see Mitzy in recovery, and Kayne spotted Taylor waiting in the empty hall.

He walked towards her, pulling the surgical cap off his head and brushing back the dark, ruffled waves of his hair. "You can relax, now," he assured her. "Everything went smoothly."

Hearing the words, she felt relief flooding through her. She let out a long sigh, not even realizing she'd been holding her breath.

"Easy," he told her. "Just take a few deep breaths."

Before she realized what was happening, Kayne drew her into a quiet corner and pulled her against him, cradling her head against his chest. "Everything's okay," he whispered against her ear, his warm breath tickling her cheek. "Sometimes the biggest shock comes after the fear has passed. It's the body's way of coping with danger."

The biggest shock, Taylor reasoned, was the way Kayne was holding her. There was no way for her body to cope with this kind of danger. When she stiffened slightly, his hands roamed across her back, her shoulders, her waist, willing her to relax. The slow, skilled stroking of his palms and fingers sent a delicious heat coursing through her veins. With her head pressed against his chest, she felt the strong warmth of him, smelled the clean spice of his aftershave, heard the fast, forceful beat of his heart.

Did he feel it too, the heady euphoria induced by

the contact between them? Or was this another routine procedure for Dr. Frost, just another chemical equation?

She tipped her head back and stared into his eyes. The smoldering look she saw there caught the breath in her throat. He *did* feel it. Kayne wasn't any more immune than she was.

With a kind of detached fascination, she watched the blue fire-and-ice kindle in his eyes. The oxygen seemed to freeze in her lungs, but it didn't matter. When he brought his mouth near hers and moved to kiss her, she forgot to breathe.

Somehow, the stress of the past weeks, the tension of last night, the anticipation of the morning, had all distilled into this one inevitable moment. She'd known all along that it would happen like this. She knew, as he bent to taste her lips, that his kiss was going to be very good, very sweet, very *right*.

"Taylor," he murmured, his cool, minty mouth only inches away. "Taylor . . ."

The rhythmic clicks of high heels approaching from down the long linoleum hall startled them both. Kayne caught himself just in time and drew back. He swore softly under his breath and with hard-won control, held Taylor at arm's length.

The sudden sense of loss left her reeling and dizzy with longing. She felt a warm flush stealing across her cheeks and raised her trembling hands to cool them.

"Oh—" purred a frigid, feminine voice behind them. "Kayne, *there* you are." This was followed by a low, throaty laugh. "I'm not *interrupting* anything, am I?"

Taylor turned at the sound of the familiar voice. It had a distinct, glassy tone to it, a cold, brilliant melody like the ringing of icicle chimes. It belonged to Kiki Vandemere.

When Taylor saw the cool, appraising look on the woman's face, her heart plummeted. As a member of the hospital board, Kiki could make serious trouble if she wanted to. And judging by the envy Taylor read in her eyes, she definitely wanted to.

Kiki's gaze swept over Taylor as if she were an annoying insect, an irritating little bug that could easily be ground to dust with the pointed toe of one designer shoe. Kiki's perfectly composed, possessive glance was aimed at Kayne. Taylor just happened to be in the way.

Kayne folded his hands behind his back and gave Kiki a swift examination. His open stare, bold and almost insolent, would have had a weaker woman running for cover. But Kiki didn't even flinch. She knew there was no reason to. Dr. Frost would need the aid of his microscope to find so much as a flaw on her.

From the sleek, pearl-trimmed coils of raven hair at her neck, to the pink, high-fashion suit that set off the delicacy of her alabaster skin, she was perfection itself.

Kayne concluded his appraisal with a look of appreciation, regarding Kiki as he might look upon an expensive piece of art. "Miss Berne and I just had some good news about a case we've been working on together."

Kiki raised one elegant eyebrow and favored Taylor with a cursory glance. "Ahhh, something to do with your little bears, I presume? Ms. Hardigree mentioned that your 'Bear Care' program is coming up for review soon.''

Taylor nodded, her agate-brown eyes suddenly sparkling with animation. ''I think you'll agree that it's a deserving cause, Mrs. Vandemere.''

Kiki smiled, but it looked as if the effort pained her. ''Call me Kiki, dear. Everyone does.'' She laughed, proudly displaying the empty ring finger of her left hand. ''Besides, I'm not a 'Mrs.' anymore.'' She flashed her brilliant green eyes in Kayne's direction.

Taylor tried to smile back, but she had to bite her tongue when Kiki placed one possessive hand on Kayne's arm.

''Really, Kayne,'' Kiki murmured in a sultry, seductive voice, pointedly ignoring Taylor's existence. ''When are you going to take me up on my offer for some rest and relaxation? I just re-decorated the beach house, and I'm dying for you to see it. Besides, you could use the time off. You haven't had a vacation for as long as I can remember.''

Kayne smiled lightly. ''I'm afraid the word 'vacation' isn't in my vocabulary, Kiki.''

This daunting reply didn't seem to faze Kiki one bit. She coyly looked away, fingering the triple-strand pearl bracelet on her delicate wrist. ''Well, if you ever change your mind. . . . '' She let her voice trail away suggestively.

Taylor cringed, embarrassed to witness such blatantly provocative behavior. Surely, Kiki could have waited until she was alone with Kayne. Or maybe she *wanted* Taylor to overhear. Was this Kiki's way of protecting her territory? Just what sort of claim did Kiki have on Kayne Frost, anyway?

Taylor stole a glance in Kayne's direction. He didn't seem to be annoyed in the least by Kiki's brash behavior. In fact, if the look of amusement on his face was anything to go by, he seemed to be enjoying it immensely.

Enough, Taylor reasoned, was enough. She cleared her throat. "Excuse me."

They both looked at her in surprise, as if suddenly remembering her existence.

"I'd better be going," she explained. "I left the gift shop unattended."

"Of course, dear," Kiki murmured, waving one jeweled hand vaguely in the air. "Run along."

Taylor turned to leave. As she was walking down the hallway, Kiki called after her, "Oh, by the way, Taylor, have you decided to sell me that wonderful bear yet? What is it you call him—Mr. Mustard?"

Taylor bit back the sharp retort that came unbidden to her lips. "His name is Mr. Marmalade," she corrected firmly. "And the answer's still no, Kiki. I'm just not interested."

Kiki returned her look with a cool smile. "Don't worry, I'm patient." She turned to Kayne. "Someday, I'm going to add that bear to my antique collection. Kayne, you really must come over to see my collection. . . ."

Taylor didn't stick around to hear the details of that invitation. She walked slowly back to the gift shop, feeling more than a little sick to her stomach. Kiki had made it abundantly clear that Kayne was the next victim on her long list of matrimonial targets. She'd divorced husband number three and was now after fresh game.

Kiki collected husbands the way she collected antiques—only the best would satisfy her. She wanted Mr. Marmalade as an expensive trophy for that costly hobby. She wanted Kayne as the ultimate trophy for her other collection. Unfortunately, the rich and beautiful Kiki usually got what she wanted.

Well, Taylor mused spitefully, she would never get Mr. Marmalade. Never. Kiki didn't want him for the right reasons. She only wanted him because of his monetary value. She couldn't see any difference between the lovable bear and one of her precious pieces of glass or porcelain. Mr. Mustard, indeed!

And as for Kayne, Kiki was welcome to him.

Here she stopped, and let a bit of honesty sink in. *Okay, Taylor*, she scolded herself. *Who are you kidding? You're half in love with the man already.*

Half in love? She slipped into the shop and closed the door behind her, breathing fast. She shook herself soundly. It couldn't be true. She was simply overreacting to the events of the morning. *Get a grip, Taylor.* A man tries to kiss you, and next you imagine you're in love with him.

She groaned and slumped onto the stool behind the counter. A hundred bears stared down at her from the shelves, their silent, searching expressions appearing to read her confusion, their calm, curious faces asking the one question she didn't want to answer. Even Mr. Marmalade, watching her from the vantage point of the cart, appeared to be quizzing her.

"Is it true?" his soft, sensitive eyes seemed to ask.

Taylor jumped up from the stool and wheeled the bear cart into the closet, closing the door firmly behind her. She leaned against it, feeling just a bit guilty for shutting her friend in the closet.

But she couldn't face him at this moment, or face the question he seemed to be asking. She wasn't ready for the answer.

Chapter 5

T aylor added an extra dollop of cream to her morning coffee, stirred in a generous sprinkling of sugar and sprawled out on the living room carpet to enjoy the Saturday morning paper. Patches eyed the coffee with cool, cat-like disdain. Cocking his head in Taylor's direction he gave her an admonishing feline stare, as if to ask, "Where's *my* cream?"

Sighing with resignation and apologizing profusely to her offended little friend, Taylor hauled herself up from a perfectly comfortable reclining position to pour Patches a small dish of cream. Her efforts did not go unrewarded.

Patches made quick work of the liquid delicacy, stopping occasionally between unfastidious slurps to lick his mouth and give Taylor several slow, adoring blinks.

Satisfied that her cat was happy, Taylor restored the cream to the refrigerator and made a second attempt to enjoy her paper. But no sooner had she managed to roll up the sleeves of her bedtime-bear bathrobe and stretch out among the pillows strewn on the floor, than the phone rang.

"Blast!" she muttered, scrambling to her feet again, leaving a trail of scattered cushions in her wake. So much for the quiet hour she'd planned. Peaceful solitude was becoming just a fond, distant memory. Her life was growing more complicated by the minute.

"Hello?" she managed, picking up the receiver on the third ring.

"Taylor? Did I wake you?" came the smooth masculine voice.

"Kayne! No, I—I've been up for hours." Since dawn, she added silently. Thinking about you.

"I didn't get a chance to talk to you again yesterday. You slipped away so fast."

She cleared her throat. "Yes, well, I understand how busy you are." Too busy, she added under her breath.

"I'd like to see you. Are you free today?"

"Today? It's Saturday." Free for what? she wondered. More consultations and observations, no doubt. More theorizing about her bear therapy. Didn't the man ever rest? Did he expect her to work all weekend, too?

"You're busy, then?" came the low response.

She detected an odd note of disappointment in his voice, an appealing tone that brought a guilty twinge to her heart. It was selfish of her to spend the day loafing if Kayne needed her input on the project. She ought to be grateful that he wanted to meet with her at all. He'd shown sincere, professional interest in her bears, setting aside his original skepticism to study their potential with an open mind. So why did his all-business attitude leave her feeling so frustrated?

"I'm not exactly busy," she told him honestly. "Just relaxing."

"Excellent. I'll stop by to pick you up."

She glanced longingly at the newspaper on the floor, the inviting mound of pillows, the rapidly cooling coffee, then answered with quiet resignation, "Oh, you don't have to bother. I can drive myself to the hospital."

"It's no bother," he informed her matter-of-factly. "I planned to get you on my way home."

"Oh." She gave the receiver a puzzled glance. On his way home?

"Any objections?"

"Well . . . " She wasn't exactly sure what she was objecting to. Was Kayne inviting her to his house? No. She must have misunderstood.

"Bring your bathing suit," he suggested. "I'll take you for a spin in my boat."

Bathing suit? He *was* inviting her over. She could hardly believe it. Not trusting her own voice, she asked, "What about the bears?"

"You can bring them, too," he laughed. "As long as they don't mind getting wet." With another good-humored laugh, he promised to be there within the hour and hung up.

Taylor replaced the receiver in a state of shock. Apparently this meeting had nothing to do with bears or business of any kind.

Taylor shook her head, trying to bring her jumbled thoughts to order. She didn't have time to think about anything right now. She had to get ready. Kayne would be at her door in less than an hour.

One glance at the comfortable confusion of her living room was enough to send her into panic. Kayne's meticulous sense of order would surely be offended by her hedonistic, harem-style pillow arrangement. She'd better modify the picture, just in case he decided to come in. Uprooting a surprised Patches from the warm, cozy spot he'd selected right in the middle of the pile, Taylor sorted the multitude of cushions, saving just a few to accent her couch with a properly conservative touch. The rest of the offending bunch she stuffed unceremoniously under the couch and out of sight.

Satisfied with her handiwork, she showered at top speed, then dried and brushed her sun-lightened hair until it shone. Towel-clad, she ransacked her dresser drawers for a swimsuit. She finally selected a simple white one-piece, a plain but flattering maillot, whose only concession to slinkiness was a dramatic cut-away back.

After slipping the suit on, Taylor examined her reflection in the mirror, and decided it was a bit too revealing. So she opted for a floral cover-up on top of the suit and a pair of pink pull-on shorts. White deck shoes that accentuated the golden tan of her legs completed the picture.

By the time she had fastened a narrow gold chain around her neck and located her pina-colada-scented sunscreen, Kayne's car had pulled into her driveway. As he stepped out of the low-slung silver vehicle, she ran out to meet him.

"Hi," she murmured, suddenly breathless. Snug jeans molded his trim, well-toned legs while a white cotton sweater with a deep v-neck and pushed-up sleeves showed a seductive sampling of his swarthy-dark skin. Sporty, mirrored sunglasses hid his eyes, but the hint of smile at the corners of his mouth was unmistakable.

He gave her a short, approving nod. "Hi, yourself."

She stepped around to the passenger side as he swung open her door. "Did you bring your suit?" he asked.

"Sure did," she told him, and raised her blouse a fraction to reveal an inch of suit. Then, realizing that her gesture might appear a bit more provocative than she'd intended and blushing at the speculative gleam of interest in his eyes, she tried to cover up her embarrassment by holding up the bottle of sunscreen. "See? I'm ready for anything."

"Anything?" he asked, a sultry, teasing note in his voice.

Taylor's heart gave a quick flutter. "Well," she added as a prudent afterthought, "almost anything."

Kayne laughed out loud and slid into the driver's side. With a simple twist of his wrist, he turned the key in the ignition and brought the engine purring to life. Taylor fastened her seat belt, settling comfortably into the plush, body-hugging seat. She willed herself to breathe normally as Kayne turned the car onto the main road, skillfully guiding the power at his fingertips with effortless control.

He kept his eyes on the road as he spoke. "I'm glad you were free today. As long as we both have the time off, I thought we might as well spend it together."

Taylor frowned slightly. "Yes, I suppose we might as well."

He shot a quick glance in her direction. "I didn't mean it that way. What I meant was," he paused, searching for the right words, "we've been working together at the hospital, but we never have time to talk. I thought this would give us a chance."

She nodded seriously, staring out the window. "Right."

When Kayne fell silent, Taylor absorbed herself in the spectacular scenery speeding by. The two-lane bridge across the St. Lucie River carried them closer to the ocean, revealing many interesting sights along the way. The sun sparkled on the water like a thousand prisms of glass flung across its surface. Local fishermen lounged against the concrete railing, waiting for a bite on their baited lines and soaking up the sun. Brown pelicans flapped in the air above with clumsy, prehistoric grace.

They sped across the causeway, a thin strip of land that snaked between two rivers, as a windsurfer sailing in the shallows of the Indian River attempted a tricky turn on his flimsy craft and made a sudden, playful crash into the water. The laughter bubbled in Taylor's throat, and Kayne turned to smile at her in shared amusement.

At that moment, Taylor realized there was no one she'd rather spend the day with than Kayne Frost. Today—for this one day—she intended to relax and to make the most of it. Because on Monday morning, or sooner if that awful beeper went off, Kayne Frost would turn back into Dr. Frost. Mr. Hyde would turn back into Dr. Jekyll.

Taylor stifled a giggle at that comparison, imagining Kayne with a mad, maniacal gleam in his eyes.

Kayne gave her a devilish glance from the corner of his eyes. "Do that again," he suggested.

She wrinkled her brow. "Do what?"

"That laugh of yours. It's wonderful. Like a breath of fresh air."

Taylor flushed and pretended to stare out the window. No man had ever told her such a thing before. "I was just thinking of something funny."

"Hmm," he commented. "You should do it more often."

He pulled the car into a long driveway overgrown with hibiscus flowers, stately queen palms, and scruffy wild palmettos. Bright birds darted through the undergrowth, feasting on fallen oranges, overripe mangoes, and yellow-gold star fruit. Taylor blinked, marveling at the wild beauty of it. Somehow, she'd expected a neat, sculptured lawn, carefully trimmed hedges, a gardener maybe. Here, at least, was a part of Kayne's life left completely unstructured, completely untamed.

He pulled up to the house, a low, tile-roofed villa clinging carelessly to a high bank overlooking the inlet to the ocean. The house spread itself through the jungle foliage like an osprey spreading its wings. When Kayne helped her out of the car and led her past the fountained patio to the front door, Taylor took a deep, intoxicating breath of ocean spray mixed with orchid-perfume. The smell reminded her of island coves, of rain forests, of moonlight.

As Kayne led her into his home, Taylor halted in

the front hall, stunned by the ocean view out of Kayne's living room. ''Oh,'' she murmured, ''it's lovely.''

He walked to the far side of the room, where the entire wall was merely one great window, and pulled back the curtains to give her a better view of the glistening water and the vast, aquamarine ocean beyond. Far below them where the calm, lazy river lapped against the sandy shore, a narrow dock jutted out into the water like a picket fence attempting to escape the boundaries of land. A slim, burnished speedboat dipped gracefully at the far end of the dock, bobbing and dancing, testing her moorings with an eager, restless energy, the way a race horse might test the strength of its reins.

''You approve?'' he asked, removing his sunglasses to reveal an expression in his eyes more unfathomable than the camouflage of the lenses.

''I—of course, it's like paradise.''

''Almost.''

She turned away from the window, noticing for the first time the furnishings, or rather the absence of them. She thought of the jumbled comfort of her own apartment, especially the pillows wrinkling under her couch, and she couldn't help noticing the contrast.

Kayne's home was spartan, decorated for form and function with little thought given to beauty or comfort. A rugged leather couch faced the window, the floor in front of it littered with medical magazines, technical trade journals and complicated computer print-outs. A single wooden chair stood next to the couch, and opposite, a wall of overstocked bookshelves nearly touched the ceiling. A grand piano dominated the corner, black and shining with sunlight reflecting off its glossy surface.

There was nothing else in the room. No plants, no paintings on the walls, no ornamentation or decoration of any kind. It had the look of a summer home abandoned by its owners during a long, cold winter. A house where the landlord spent little time within the confines of its walls.

Taylor fought the odd, lonely feeling that settled in the pit of her stomach. She walked over to the piano, and she ran her fingers lightly over the keys, aware that Kayne was watching.

''You play?'' she asked, then blushed at the foolishness of her question. This piano, with its mellow ivory keys and time-polished edges, was obviously not just for decoration.

Kayne inclined his head in acknowledgement. ''A little,'' came his cryptic response.

Taylor turned back to the windowed wall, unable to take her eyes from the view for very long. She could picture Kayne out on his boat in the evenings, skimming across the water with his strong, capable hands in control of the wheel, with nothing but his unflinching confidence and an early star to guide him. She could imagine him walking about the grounds, clearing his mind of the daily burdens he faced, and later, falling asleep on the couch, a medical magazine still resting on his chest. Maybe this house suited him, after all.

When Kayne disappeared into the back room, Taylor settled down on the couch, content to watch the scenic picture of the tropics unfold beyond the window. She was still lost in the beauty of it when he returned a few minutes later.

"Ready?" his voice sounded behind her.

"Hmmm?" she sighed, still drinking in the scenery.

"For a ride," he explained, walking around to stand directly in front of her. He was wearing swimming trunks and carried a bottle of his own sunscreen and a towel. "You're not the only one who's prepared."

Taylor gulped, unable to pull her eyes away from his perfectly proportioned body.

"Come on, you're going to love it," Kayne insisted, and took her by the hand.

I love it already, she thought to herself and followed him out onto the back patio and down the white brick steps that led to the dock.

After he helped her onto the boat, Kayne made preparations to launch the craft, freeing the trim fiberglass hull from the restraint of its mooring ropes. Taylor shielded her eyes from the sun and studied Kayne in action.

What was wrong with her? Why wouldn't her eyes function normally and respond to what her brain was telling them? She was sick, no doubt, with a bad case of something. If that something was love, she intended to get over it, because it was definitely driving her stark, raving mad.

"Ready to cast off?" he asked, almost as an afterthought. Before his words were out, the propeller roared to life.

Taylor sank into her seat and gripped the armrest with grim intensity.

"Relax," Kayne told her. "You're in safe hands."

Safe? She didn't doubt the skill of those hands for an instant, but there was nothing safe about sharing close quarters with Kayne. She'd known, from the first moment of attraction between them, that she would never be safe again. Not when he was nearby. Not when her heart sent the craziest kind of feelings to her fuzzied brain.

Or was her brain sending signals to her heart? Whatever the correct medical explanation, she still knew how it felt. Terrible. Wonderful. And a little bit of everything in between.

As the boat gathered speed, Taylor gradually released her hold on the armrest and began to enjoy the ride. The sun on her face, warming her, gave her a primitive sense of joy. The wind, whipping her hair into untamed disarray, made her feel free and wild. An hour later, he'd put the boat through its paces and had given her the ride of her life. She felt radiant and her spirits soared.

When he finally pulled the craft into a secluded cove, cutting the motor to keep from disturbing any wildlife along the shore, she leaned back in her seat, giddy and exhilarated.

"Don't stop!" she exclaimed.

He grinned, his eyes glittering with amusement. "Somehow, I knew you'd love it. You're just a child at heart, aren't you, Taylor? A free spirit."

She stammered, confused by the tone of his voice. "I—I'm no child, Kayne."

"Don't get me wrong," he explained. "I admire that wide-eyed innocence of yours. There aren't many

people who approach life on such simple, uncompli-
cated terms.''

"Life doesn't have to be difficult," she said stub-
bornly.

"No," he agreed, "but it can be very complicated.
Sometimes, situations arise that don't have an easy
solution. Some problems can't be solved by a hug from
a Teddy bear.''

She shrugged. "Bears can't take the place of sound,
medical solutions, but they can give some measure of
comfort. They can listen to problems and return love
without reservation. They can help people to express
their feelings.''

He shook his head. "Feelings," he told her, "can't
always be trusted. They might be too strong," he said,
looking intently into her eyes, "or too uncertain," he
added, looking away to the shoreline. "I've learned to
rely on facts instead.''

Taylor had the distinct impression that he wasn't
talking about medicine at all. But before she could
respond, he changed the subject.

"Which reminds me," he said, giving her a stern,
professional look. "As the attending physician in
charge here, I feel personally responsible for your wel-
fare." He tapped the end of her nose with his fingertip.
"You're getting too much sun. It may be winter, but
the ultraviolet intensity is still strong. Put on that sunscreen you brought.''

Taylor gave him a sweet, obedient smile. "I always
follow doctor's orders.''

He quirked one eyebrow in faint amusement. "I may
remind you of that someday.''

Pointedly ignoring his remark, Taylor located her suntan lotion and proceeded to slather it on her face and arms. She removed her blouse and shorts to keep the coconut-sweet, sticky liquid from staining her clothes, but carefully averted her eyes from Kayne as she did so. She didn't want him to see the blush creeping across her cheeks. He'd already described her as a child, for goodness sake. If he noticed that she was embarrassed to be seen in a bathing suit, he would never let her live it down.

But he didn't say a word as she spread the creamy, scented liquid on one leg, and then the other. Encouraged by his sudden, unexplained silence, she handed him the bottle and asked him to rub some on her back. He *was* a doctor, after all. What was another body in a bathing suit to him? Probably just a lot of flesh and tissue.

"Do you mind?" she asked.

Kayne choked back a small sound, but managed to nod, indicating his willingness to oblige. He set his jaw a little tighter than usual and squared his shoulders as he took the bottle from her and began to spread the lotion on her back.

His fingers glided over the smooth surface of her skin, pressing lightly, feathering softly across her waist and shoulders with careful control.

"Mmm . . . " she murmured, relaxing her back in involuntary response.

Kayne's hands stiffened and went suddenly still.

"What is it?" she asked, turning her head to glance into his eyes. They were heavy, hooded, and smoldering with emotion.

"It's getting late," he responded, drawing his hands away as if he didn't dare touch her again. "We'd better be getting back."

Not wanting to argue or probe any further, Taylor stowed the bottle of lotion and sank back into her seat.

They rode back to the house in silence, Kayne's face revealing little of what he was thinking, Taylor's thoughts turned inward. What had she done or said, to evoke such a response from him?

Just when things were going so well, when they'd started to share something other than work. Was that it? Was Kayne unwilling to share too much of himself outside of his job? Maybe he intended to keep their relationship on a professional level. Maybe inviting her here had been a terrible mistake.

They made their way back inside the house, the awful silence still surrounding them. Kayne vanished into the kitchen while Taylor, her heart heavy with disappointment, slumped onto the piano bench and fingered the keys distractedly.

The random notes brought an immediate response from Kayne, who called to her from the next room. "That's awful," he groaned. "Like the mating call of a sea monster."

Relieved to have drawn any reaction from him at all, Taylor continued her unskilled plunking at the keys, striving for more discord than before. Anything to break the somber mood.

Kayne returned from the kitchen, carrying drinks, but he set them down immediately, moving his hands to a protective position over his ears. "You're terrible," he told her, a hint of amusement in his aqua eyes. "Possibly the worst I've ever heard."

She smiled, stood up from her position at the bench, and gave him a formal bow. "Thank you, maestro. Now it's your turn." She gestured to the keyboard, and then to the empty room beyond. "Your audience awaits."

He rubbed one hand thoughtfully against his chin. "How flattering. An audience of one."

She laughed. "Please Kayne, play something for me."

His smile, as warm as a caress, sent her heart dancing with excitement. "For you, Taylor, anything."

He took her hand and led her back to the piano bench, settling so close beside her that she had to fight the overwhelming urge to lean her head on his shoulder, to snuggle against him.

"What would you like to hear?" she heard him ask.

She tried to clear her head of all extraneous thoughts and concentrate on music. Yes, music. But at the moment, she couldn't think of a single tune.

He ran his fingers over the keyboard, testing notes here and there. "Yes?" he urged, his expression a study in patience.

Taylor tried not to stare at his hands. Strong, capable hands that were now moving skillfully over the keys in a silky, sultry melody, pulling life from the instrument as surely as he pulled an emotional response from her.

"Something like this?" he suggested, then lost himself in the music, concentrating only on the sound, the rhythm of the notes and the sweet, haunting harmony.

Taylor, too, was swept away by the music, by the mellow tune that made her think of the ocean, of songs sung by sailors at sea, of whales, or mermaids perhaps. She closed her eyes, allowing the delicious feeling to float around her. When Kayne finished playing, the house fell silent except for the soft lapping of waves against the shore below.

"That was beautiful," she sighed. "Where did you learn to play like that?"

Kayne flexed his fingers, limbering up the muscles, testing for strength. "When I was younger," he told her, "I had a promising career ahead of me as a concert pianist. But I was too young and foolish to appreciate the gift I had. I nearly threw it away."

Taylor stared at him with growing curiosity. "What happened? It's hard to imagine you doing anything foolish."

He laughed softly, clenching and unclenching his right fist, staring at the jagged scar across the back of his hand. "Everyone's had an episode or two in their lives they're not especially proud of. Mine happened at the ripe old age of fifteen, when I imagined that the world was mine for the taking."

Taylor didn't speak, but their eyes met and locked for a moment and she waited patiently for him to continue.

"I studied piano throughout my childhood," he explained. "Everyone had high hopes that I would continue in music. I expected to myself. I was ready to prove to the world what a wonderful talent I had. But one sunny afternoon, everything changed." He held up his hand. "I injured myself. Very seriously."

"How?"

"Stupidity," he said, shaking his head, "sheer, careless stupidity. I was mowing lawns to pick up some extra cash, and my hand made accidental contact with a lawnmower blade. The worst part," he continued, "was knowing that the accident was my own fault, that I wasn't as invulnerable as I'd believed. They rushed me to the hospital, and it looked like my exalted career was over before it had begun."

"I don't understand," Taylor said, "your hand works perfectly."

"I was lucky," he admitted. "There was a surgeon at the hospital who managed to save my hand. Eventually, after many months of physical therapy, I was playing again, better than ever."

Taylor gave him a puzzled look. "So why did you give up music?"

"I didn't give it up," he told her. "I found something better."

"Medicine," she stated flatly.

"Medicine," he agreed. "After that incident, I couldn't stop thinking about the surgeon who saved my hand and the marvelous ability it took. Later, I went back to see him at the hospital and listened to everything he was willing to share with me about his work. He had helped so many people and made such an important difference in their lives. His skill really mattered. I was determined to try it myself, to see if I could master medicine as well as music."

Taylor nodded in simple understanding. "Your work means so much to you."

His eyes looked directly into hers. "It does."

Touched by the emotion in his voice and that he'd shared the episode with her, Taylor reached out and tenderly laid her own small hand across his scarred one. "Kayne," she whispered, gathering her courage before it slipped away again. "Why did you invite me here?"

He gave her a wry smile. "Maybe I wanted to prove I don't have icewater in my veins."

A slap would have hurt her less than the sting of his words. For the first time, Taylor realized she'd caused him pain.

"Kayne," she choked, "I'm sorry I ever said that, I—"

"Forget it," he told her in a harsh, clipped tone. "I'm well aware of my stone-hearted reputation." He laughed, but the sound was cold, mechanical. "It's appropriate for a heart surgeon, don't you think? I guess I've earned it."

Taylor wanted to reach out, to say she'd exaggerated before, that she never really meant it. She wanted to say *something*, but no words would come.

He gave her a scornful glance. "Don't look at me that way. I don't want your pity."

"What do you want?" she cried, anguish shattering the last remnants of her control.

He clamped his free hand over her wrist and pulled her toward him. A moment later she was in his arms.

"This," he muttered as he moved to kiss her. "I want this."

Chapter 6

Taylor lifted her hands to his head with every intention of pushing him away. Instead, she wound her fingers through the dark waves of his hair and kissed him back.

She thrilled to the silent melody as he lowered his head and buried himself in the nape of her neck, raining cool, light kisses along the base of her throat.

"Kayne," she whispered.

Suddenly he pushed her away, drawing air sharply into his lungs as he fought to steady himself. "No," he told her, white-hot emotion in his eyes. "We don't need this kind of complication."

Complication. There it was again, that awful, insidious little word. The word Kayne had used to describe her from the start. This time it hit Taylor like a bucket of cold water, chilling the blood in her veins. He didn't feel any differently about her now than he had then. To Dr. Kayne Frost, she was just a complication and an unwanted one at that.

She pulled herself away from his grasp, fighting for composure. "You're absolutely right," she agreed quietly. "We don't need any complications."

Kayne let out a hoarse sigh. "Taylor. Let me explain."

She tried to smile. "Forget it."

He gave her a harsh laugh. "I can't forget it. Not any more than I've been able to forget you. But it wouldn't work between us. My job, my patients—there's just no room for anything more than a part-time relationship. With you, Taylor, part-time wouldn't be enough."

She nodded, fighting back the lump in her throat, wishing that he wouldn't say any more. She couldn't bear to hear another word. The hardest part was knowing he was right. There was no future for them together.

Hadn't she promised herself never to get involved with a doctor, to never make the same mistake her mother made? Every time Kayne's blasted beeper went off, she would feel the same familiar pain—the pain of desertion, of aching loneliness.

She'd been foolish to imagine, even for a moment, that it could be otherwise. Even if he did want to change his lifestyle enough to make room for a woman, she could never be that woman. She'd known from the beginning that Kayne Frost was not the right man for her.

She gave him a brittle smile. "Drive me home?"

Kayne frowned, but he didn't argue. He led her out to the car and they rode back to her apartment in virtual silence. When he let her off at her door, he bent to drop a light kiss on her nose. "See you at the hospital."

"Right," she responded softly. "At the hospital."

* * *

"Cough, Mitzy," encouraged Taylor, "don't be afraid to cough."

From the pillow-filled comfort of her hospital bed, Mitzy responded with several promising sounds.

"Good girl," Taylor told her. "Now try to cough a little louder."

Mitzy rolled her eyes and shot Taylor a look of petulant exasperation. "It hurts," she insisted.

Taylor's heart constricted in her chest, then swelled with sympathy for the child. Mitzy had been through a lot in her five short years, the latest bad luck being her recent development of pneumonia. But she was well on her way to recovery, if she would only co-operate a little more.

Kayne had instructed Mitzy to cough frequently, as part of the therapy to clear her respiratory passages. But getting a willful young lady to cough against her wishes, especially when it hurt, was no easy task. The nurses had all but given up. Because of her previous experience with Mitzy, Taylor had decided to lend a hand. So far, she'd met with only limited success.

"Please, Mitzy," she almost begged. "Just a little more."

Mitzy frowned, refusing to look in Taylor's direction. "No."

Taylor picked Mitzy's bear off the nightstand and gave it a squeeze, as if she could extract the help she needed from his limp, furry body. She laid him on the bed next to Mitzy. "If you won't do it for me, Mitzy, will you at least cough for Elwin?"

Mitzy peered at the bear from the corner of her eye,

trying to decide if he was really worth it. She made a small, choking sound.

Encouraged, Taylor placed the bear on Mitzy's chest. "Hold him tight, Mitzy, and every time it hurts, just squeeze really hard."

Mitzy wrapped her arms around Elwin and let out another, stronger cough.

"Good!" Taylor exclaimed. "Now don't let him go, Mitzy, and keep it up."

To Taylor's amazement, Mitzy obeyed, emitting a loud, ugly hacking noise. To Taylor, it was the most beautiful sound in the world.

Even more encouraging was the fact that Mitzy didn't seem to be in as much pain. The bear distracted her, giving her something to focus on, something other than her own physical feelings.

"Now, why didn't I think of that?"

Taylor whirled around to see Kayne standing in the doorway. "Oh! Hello, Dr. Frost."

He nodded, crossing the room to Mitzy's bed. "Good morning." He turned to the child. "Keep up the good work, Mitzy."

Mitzy smiled and rewarded Kayne's praises with another loud clearing of her throat.

Kayne turned his attention to Taylor. "Are you free for lunch?"

She gave him a doubtful look. Since the incident at his house last week, she'd tried to avoid being alone with him. But their close collaboration with the patients made it virtually impossible. Lunch with Kayne would make it even harder to keep her distance.

"There's an idea I'd like to discuss with you," he added, "about the bears."

The suggestion seemed harmless. If she could only keep her mind on work and away from him. "All right," she agreed. "Shall I meet you in the cafeteria?"

He glanced at his watch. "Fine. Say one o'clock?"

Taylor nodded and slipped away. When the time arrived to meet him, she made her way through the short food line to select her meal, then located a booth at the corner of the room where they could have relative peace and quiet. She didn't have long to wait. Kayne arrived minutes later, bearing his own tray and sank into the seat beside her.

"Mystery meat again," he muttered, glancing down at his tray with obvious disgust. But when he raised his eyes to hers, there was a good-natured grin on his face. "It's just as well. I don't think I'd recognize a home-cooked meal if I saw one."

If we were together, Taylor thought, I'd remedy that immediately. I'd feed him the way a hard-working man deserves to be fed. I'd show him how good a home-cooked meal can taste.

She stared down at the salad on her plate. If he was mine, she thought dizzily, I'd make a wonderful home for him, with delicious smells coming from the kitchen, pictures hung on every wall, and happy, grimy children playing Tarzan in our jungle yard.

"You don't look too impressed with that salad, either," he commented, drawing her out of her pleasant reverie.

"I guess I don't have much of an appetite today."

He pushed his tray aside. "Neither do I."

"Maybe we should just get down to business," she suggested. The sooner the better. No telling what direction her wandering brain would follow next.

She pulled herself out of the daydream and forced her mind to concentrate on what Kayne was saying.

"I was very impressed with Mitzy's progress," he explained. "Hugging that bear to her chest when she coughs is obviously helping her cope with the pain."

Taylor perked up at Kayne's comment. He was finally beginning to see the merit of the bears. In this way, at least, the time they'd spent together was paying off.

"It gave me an idea," he told her, "to develop a bear of our own, a respiratory therapy bear specifically designed to help patients recovering from heart, abdominal, or thoracic surgery."

Taylor raised her eyebrows and listened with growing interest.

"If we made the bear flatter," he suggested, "more pillow-shaped, it would help protect and strengthen any surgical incisions as the patient coughed." He took a pen from his pocket and made a cursory sketch on his paper napkin, then thrust it toward her. "Something like this."

She leaned in for a closer inspection of the design. It certainly looked simple enough. If other patients reacted as positively as Mitzy, the bear would be a sure success.

"What do you think?" Kayne asked, "Can you sew one up based on a drawing like that? Make us an experimental prototype bear?"

Taylor nodded enthusiastically. "It's a wonderful

idea. Sure to make any patient's recovery more 'bear-able'!'' She gave Kayne a humorous smile, then took another look at the drawing. ''But the arms aren't right.'' She took the pen from Kayne's hand and made a few changes of her own. ''There,'' she exclaimed with satisfaction. ''He needed wider arms, for better hugging capacity.''

Kayne smiled a heart-stopping, tummy-tightening smile that sent a warm shiver straight to her toes. ''You're definitely an expert in the good hugs department,'' he told her.

Taylor felt the warm blush stealing across her cheeks, but was saved by the timely appearance of Ms. Hardigree. The older woman waved to them from across the room and made her way to their table, trying to balance a heavily laden tray in one hand and an oversized, overflowing leather briefcase in the other.

Kayne stood as she approached, relieving her of the tray and placing it safely on their table.

''Thank you, Dr. Frost,'' she said, slipping into the seat across from them. She patted the back of her too-tight bun, checking for any hairs that might have strayed. She nodded to Taylor. ''How are you dear? You look a bit flushed.''

Her comment only increased the color in Taylor's cheeks, but she didn't offer an explanation.

Ms. Hardigree glanced in Kayne's direction. ''Oh,'' she mumbled, as if suddenly remembering something. ''Yes, well, it is very warm in here, isn't it? Now tell me, you two, how is the bear research coming along?'' She gave Kayne a searching look. ''Is everything working out to your satisfaction, Dr. Frost? Have you had a chance to discover Miss Berne's talents yet?''

Kayne, who had settled back in his seat and was sipping a cup of coffee, nearly choked on the liquid. He made a valiant attempt to swallow. "Not entirely," he answered, recovering smoothly from the momentary surprise and staring with some amusement at Taylor, "but I'm working on it."

Ms. Hardigree's eyebrows shot up. "Indeed? Well, I'm sure you'll find the research to be very gratifying."

Taylor stared at her untouched salad and wished she was under the table.

"The preliminary research has been very," he cleared his throat, "gratifying."

"So you're beginning to see some merit in the bears?" Ms. Hardigree asked.

Kayne coughed softly. "Oh, yes—the bears."

Ms. Hardigree crunched away at the croutons on her salad. "I'm glad to hear it. I'll look forward to hearing about your findings at the board meeting."

Taylor risked a glance in Ms. Hardigree's direction. "Is it still scheduled for the twenty-seventh?"

Ms. Hardigree nodded firmly. "About a week after the hospital ball." She looked from Taylor to Kayne and back again. "You *are* coming to the ball, aren't you? It's *the* event of the Christmas season."

Taylor didn't answer. She didn't think it was appropriate to attend such a fancy, charitable event alone, and since no one had asked her, she hadn't given the matter too much thought.

Ms. Hardigree gave Kayne a piercing look. "It's especially important for *you* to attend, Dr. Frost. All of the hospital's biggest sponsors will be there, making pledges for your new echocardiogram machine.'' She shot him a honey-sweet smile. ''Do you have a date yet?''

Now Taylor really wanted to sink under the table or simply crawl into a hole and hide. She could guess what was coming next in Ms. Hardigree's not-so-subtle speech.

''You don't have a date either, do you, Taylor?'' Ms. Hardigree prompted relentlessly.

Taylor cringed and took a very strong interest in her wilting salad. ''No, I—''

''If you'll excuse me, ladies,'' Kayne interrupted, saving her the trouble of a reply, ''I'm scheduled for the OR in five minutes.'' He turned to Taylor. ''You'll get started on the new project?''

She nodded. ''Right away.''

Kayne gave Ms. Hardigree a mischevious grin. ''And I *will* be attending the ball. If you'll ask the committee to save me two tickets? Excellent.'' And with that intriguing comment, he left.

''Well!'' Ms. Hardigree mused, staring at Taylor. ''You've made remarkable progress so far, dear. Remarkable.''

Taylor smiled. ''Yes, I've had some success with the bears.''

Ms. Hardigree smiled in sudden surprise. ''Oh—of course. With those too.''

Taylor guided the thick, plush fabric beneath the needle of the sewing machine, not daring to breathe. Only when the seam was finished and the two pieces firmly joined, did she finally exhale and lean back in her chair to survey the results. Not bad, she decided, but not that good either.

She tossed the would-be bear arm into the growing reject pile that littered the floor of her apartment. With the help of Patches, who regarded the whole bear-making project as a game designed solely for his entertainment, the pieces of fake-fur fabric and stuffing now spread from the top cushions on the couch to the farthest corners of the living room. The energetic cat pounced on the latest scrap with cunning enthusiasm and bravely wrestled it into submission.

Taylor shook her head in frustration. This simple project was turning into a complicated mess. Making the prototype bear shouldn't be so difficult. If she could only keep her mind on the work.

But the visions of Teddy bears dancing in her head had a peculiar way of changing to real people dancing at the holiday ball. And among those people was Kiki Vandemere, swaying seductively in the arms of Dr. Frost.

Taylor groaned and dropped to the floor, wrestling playfully with Patches. "Is that what he meant, Patches?" she asked softly. "Does he mean to take Kiki to the ball?"

Patches unsheathed his claws and tugged harder at the scrap, his tail swishing with excitement.

"Yes, she *is* very beautiful," Taylor continued, "but she's already had three husbands. Does she really need *another* one?"

Patches rolled onto his back and brought his rear paws into the action.

"You're right," she sighed, "I'm just torturing my-self. I have to stop thinking about it."

Patches gave up the fight, relaxed his forepaws against her and purred like crazy.

Taylor picked him up and held him close to her cheek. "At least I've got you, old boy."

When the doorbell rang, Patches leapt from her arms and ran expectantly to the door. Taylor stood up, brushed the fur from her jeans and went to answer it.

"Nita!" she exclaimed, "Am I glad to see you. Come on in before Patches decides to explore the great outdoors."

Nita stepped inside, took one quick look around the apartment and turned to Taylor in some amazement. "I thought I left my kids at home."

"Very funny," Taylor retorted. "Actually, I created this mess all by myself." She glanced at Patches. "Al-most."

Nita flipped her long braid over one shoulder and strolled to the couch. She pushed a pile of white fiberfill stuffing to one side and settled back against the cush-ions. "Okay," she said expectantly, "what gives?"

Taylor positioned herself in the chair at the sewing machine, bracing for a stern lecture. "The bear's not going very well," she explained, hoping Nita would let it rest with that. But her friend was genuinely con-cerned and would not be put off so easily.

"This hasn't got anything to do with Teddy bears and you know it. Taylor, you've been acting weird for weeks now. Are you going to tell me what's going on, or do I have to pry it out of you?"

Taylor bit her bottom lip and looked away. How

could she explain her feelings to Nita when she could hardly understand them herself?

"It's Frost, isn't it? He's giving you a hard time again."

Taylor blinked in surprise. She started to protest, but Nita stopped her.

"That's it, right? Drat the man, Taylor, doesn't he have anything better to do than pick on a nice person like you? Why don't you just tell him to leave you alone?"

Because I don't want him to leave me alone, Taylor admitted silently. She shrugged. "It's not what you think."

Nita narrowed her eyes. "Oh no? Then why do you jump like that every time I mention his name?"

Taylor flushed to the roots of her hair. "Do I?" she whispered.

Nita nodded, then slowly sat up a little straighter on the couch. "Taylor, you're not falling—" she broke off, her mouth gaping. "You *are*. You're attracted to him, aren't you?"

Taylor folded her hands in her lap. "I'm afraid it's more serious than that," she admitted.

Nita shook her head. "Not that I blame you. I've only seen him a couple of times around the hospital, and he always seemed pretty preoccupied, but he *is* handsome. I can't believe I didn't see this coming. . . . " She hesitated, scratching her chin. "Come to think of it, it's not such a crazy thought after all. In fact, it's perfect! Taylor, you're absolutely perfect for him." She grinned. "So it's getting serious, huh?"

Taylor shifted in her seat. "Not *that* kind of serious.

What I meant was, my feelings for him are more serious. They go beyond attraction into something, well, something more.''

Nita widened her eyes. ''Why, Taylor,'' she whispered, ''you're in love.''

Taylor swallowed hard. ''This, too, shall pass.''

''Not likely! Anyway, why would you want it to? Being in love is delicious. Better than chocolate. Better than anything.''

Taylor felt the tears prickling the back of her eyes.

''Unless, of course,'' Nita continued, ''he doesn't feel the same?''

Taylor nodded, miserable.

''I don't believe it!'' Nita protested. ''I know you said Frost is difficult to please, but is he a complete fool? That's what he'd have to be to miss out on a treasure like you.''

Taylor gave her friend a teary smile. ''Oh, there's a fool involved, but it isn't Frost.''

Nita scoffed. ''Impossible! He just hasn't come to his senses yet.''

But that was just the problem. Kayne was far too sensible where she was concerned. He was capable of making a calm, rational decision about their relationship, whereas she was knocked completely senseless by her feelings for him and had been willing to throw caution to the wind. He, on the other hand, had the good *sense* to keep this ''complication'' out of his busy life.

Taylor wiped her eyes. ''I'm just feeling sorry for myself. Probably because this project isn't going so well.''

Nita surveyed the room again. "So I noticed." She rolled up her sleeves. "Well, that's what I came for. Just tell me what I can do to help and we'll have that bear whipped into shape in no time!"

Three hours later, the bear was finished. With a sigh of gratitude and relief, Taylor sent Nita back to her family and proceeded to clean up the mess. When the doorbell rang only minutes later, she wondered what Nita had left behind.

"You're getting to be as absent-minded as I am!" she teased, opening the door. But the words froze in the air. It wasn't Nita she was speaking to, but Kayne.

He raised one curious eyebrow. "Indeed? I don't think that's possible."

Taylor took a step backward. "Oh! It's you."

He smiled. "Disappointed? May I come in anyway?"

"Of course." She stepped aside, and when his back was to her, she made a futile attempt to brush the fur debris from her blouse and jeans.

He turned and caught her in the act. "You missed a spot."

She spread her hands wide and looked down at her clothes. "Where?"

He reached out and pulled a stray tuft of fur from the sandy waves of her hair. "Here," he said, letting it drift to the floor. His hand lingered in her hair a moment, smoothing one untamed strand.

"Soft," he murmured.

"What?" she asked, nearly breathless.

"Your hair, it's so . . . soft."

Her eyes twinkled up at him. "Like bear fur?"

He brushed a wave from her face. "No. Like silk."

Taylor swallowed, and willed her heart to stop pounding so fast. Something rubbed against her ankles, and she glanced down. The spell was broken. Patches.

"Good grief, what *is* it?"

Taylor's eyes sparkled with laughter. "Don't insult Patches, he's very sensitive."

"For obvious reasons," Kayne added dryly.

She picked the animal up and mischievously deposited him in Kayne's arms. "Here. Rub him behind the ears and he'll be your friend for life."

Kayne gave the cat a doubtful glance. "Is that a recommendation or a warning?"

Patches ignored the insult and relaxed against Kayne's broad chest, letting his four great paws sprawl haphazardly.

"See?" Taylor asked, warm amusement in her tawny eyes. "He likes you."

Kayne rolled his eyes expressively, but he didn't put Patches down. He rubbed him gently under the chin and walked across the room. "You've been busy," he said, turning to Taylor.

She nodded. "I just finished the prototype bear." She indicated the sewing machine table where the newly made Teddy reclined in a basket of thread.

Kayne set Patches back on the floor and moved to examine the bear. "Excellent," he commented. "Exactly what I had in mind."

Taylor let out a sudden sigh of relief. "I saved the pattern. If you like, I can make up a few more samples to give to the patients."

Kayne nodded. "That'll be just fine." He returned

the bear to its position on the table. "I didn't expect you to finish it so fast. In fact, one reason I stopped by was to try to lend you a hand." He gave her an apologetic smile. "Apparently, I'm too late."

Taylor shook her head. "Well, thanks anyway." She hesitated, suddenly curious. "What was the other reason?"

He stepped closer and circled her waist with his hands. "To ask you a question."

Taylor's heart thumped erratically. "A question?"

Kayne smiled easily. "Relax. It won't be difficult to answer. A simple yes or no will do."

She didn't say a word, only held her breath.

Kayne's aqua eyes gleamed down at her with faint amusement. "The question is, may I take you to the hospital ball?"

Chapter 7

" "T he holiday ball?" Taylor repeated. "You want to take me?"

Kayne smiled and pulled her close. "You. Nobody else."

Taylor peeped up at him. "What about Kiki?"

He gave her a puzzled look. "Kiki Vandemere? What about her?"

"Well, I thought—I thought you might take her."

Kayne shook his head. "Not a chance. Kiki knows a great deal about hospital business, but business is as far as our relationship goes."

Joy bubbled in Taylor's heart. Kayne wasn't even interested in Kiki. Maybe, just maybe, he was actually interested in *her*.

"Well?" Kayne asked.

"Hmm?"

He gave her a playful tap on the cheek. "Well, don't keep me in suspense. Is it yes or no?"

Her eyes grew wide. "Oh! It's yes. Of course, it's yes."

He laughed and spun her around the room. "Excellent. You can dance, can't you?"

117

Taylor tried to catch her breath as the walls twirled past her in a dizzy blur. "I—I think so. It's been a while."

He swept her across the floor, gliding smoothly over the carpet and around the couch. Patches watched from the safety of the cushions, regarding this strange human ritual with wise, agate eyes.

"You haven't forgotten how to dance," Kayne whispered in her ear, dipping her low to the floor.

Taylor felt her hair tumbling about her face, the warm, confident pressure of Kayne's hands against her body. "No," she gasped. "I guess I haven't forgotten." But dancing had never been like this. This was not a bland, weary waltz, but sweet, exquisite fun. If only it would last. . . .

He pulled her closer, stopping suddenly. The short, quick sound of his breathing matched her own. "Your pulse is very fast, Taylor."

She took a few deep breaths, trying to hide her confusion. "All that dancing. I'm not used to it."

He searched her with his eyes.

She brushed the hair back from her face, noticing with some surprise that her hand was trembling. She forced a laugh. "I—I'm fine, really."

Kayne released her. "Are you? Well, maybe we should save the dancing for the ball."

Taylor nodded in relief, but her hands were still quivering, very slightly. *It's from the dancing*, she told herself. That's all, just the dancing.

But the more she tried to deny it, the more obvious the truth became. It wasn't just her hands that were affected. It was her heart and her soul that were shaken.

And the cause was not, as she'd tried to explain, from dancing.

She'd developed another side-effect from the dreaded Dr. Frost disease—the most dangerous side-effect of all—love. And that was one ailment she would never get over. There was no cure.

"Thank goodness you're here, Taylor," Ms. Hardigree exclaimed, pushing a path through the overflowing stacks of used clothes and cardboard boxes. "I need help!"

Taylor threaded her way through Ms. Hardigree's garage, marveling at the wide assortment of merchandise donated for the Stuart Hospital Annual Holiday Auction. The yearly charity event was only a week away, scheduled for the day after the ball, and the contributions, which included everything from furniture to fishing poles, needed sorting, cleaning, and tagging.

Taylor swallowed, somewhat daunted by the overwhelming task ahead. "Am I the only volunteer?" she asked doubtfully.

Ms. Hardigree smiled. "Certainly not! But you are the earliest. Why don't you come into the house for a cup of coffee before we get started? It's the least I can offer you for donating your Saturday morning."

Taylor followed her gratefully into the house. A few minutes later she was seated at the counter of a cozy kitchen, cradling a warm, steaming cup between her hands and munching contentedly on Christmas cookies.

Ms. Hardigree settled into the stool beside her. "I've been meaning to congratulate you on your fine work with little Mitzy Pearl,'' she said. ''She's finally gone home to finish her recovery.''

Taylor held a gingerbread elf poised in mid-air. ''She has? Kayne—er, Dr. Frost didn't tell me.''

Ms. Hardigree gave her a penetrating look. ''He didn't? Well, don't be too hard on him, Taylor. Mitzy's parents insisted on taking the child home earlier than expected. And Frost has been very busy this past week.''

Taylor nodded, thoughtful. Since Kayne had asked her to the ball last weekend, she'd had only quick glimpses of him in the halls. A flash of white coat, a streak of dark hair, a fleeting smile. Nothing more.

What else had she expected? The man wasn't going to change his entire lifestyle simply because he'd asked her out on a date. She wouldn't want him to. Too many patients depended on his skill and hard work.

''I understand how busy he is,'' Taylor said quietly.

Ms. Hardigree frowned. ''A little too busy, as we both know, but I don't think that will last forever. He'll self-destruct if he keeps up this pace for too long. Sooner or later, he'll figure that out for himself. In the meantime,'' she paused significantly, ''has he asked you to the ball yet?''

Taylor nearly fell off her stool. Leave it to Ms. Hardigree to be blatantly direct. ''Yes, as a matter of fact, he has.''

Ms. Hardigree clapped her hands in satisfaction. ''Marvelous! That's perfectly marvelous, dear.'' She brushed a few crumbs from the counter. ''For a while there, I was just a bit concerned about Kiki Vandemere.'' She gave Taylor a conspiratorial grin. ''But only a little. And it certainly doesn't matter now. So, have you decided what you're going to wear?''

Taylor frowned. ''I haven't really had time to go shopping. I was thinking about making the dress myself.''

Ms. Hardigree raised her eyebrows. ''My dear! The ball's only a week away. There simply isn't time for that.''

Taylor bit her lower lip. ''To be honest, Ms. Hardigree, I'm not sure I can afford the kind of gown everyone else will be wearing. I imagine they can be pretty expensive.''

Ms. Hardigree pursed her mouth, thinking rapidly. ''I have an idea. That is, if you don't mind.'' She slipped off the stool and patted Taylor on the arm. ''Wait right here, I'll show you.''

She disappeared and returned a few minutes later, carrying a large flat box, cream and gold and tied with smooth satin ribbons. She beckoned Taylor to sit beside her on the couch.

''This,'' she said, carefully unwrapping the time-worn bows, ''was a party dress I purchased many, many years ago.'' She smiled fondly. ''When I was only twenty-one.''

She lifted the lid and folded back the brittle tissue to reveal a slim confection of a dress, all smooth-flowing satin lines, embroidered finely with tiny seed pearls, shimmering sequins, and lace.

''Oh!'' Taylor exclaimed, reaching out to touch the gown in involuntary response. ''It's lovely. Ms. Hardigree, where did you wear it?''

The older woman gave her a poignant smile. ''I

never did. I planned to wear it to a college dance, but my boyfriend jilted me, you see.''

Taylor blinked in sympathy. ''How awful for you.''

Ms. Hardigree looked away, remembering. ''It was. At the time. But looking back, I realize it all worked out for the best.'' She fingered the dress tenderly. ''I wouldn't have done the gown justice anyway. You will.''

Taylor blinked. ''Beg your pardon?''

''I'd like you to have it, Taylor. To wear to the holiday ball.''

''Oh, Ms. Hardigree, I couldn't.'' She shook her head slowly, then a delighted grin stole across her face. ''Could I?''

Ms. Hardigree nodded. ''You could, and you will.'' She shook the dress out thoroughly and held it up to Taylor's face. ''It's going to be perfect. I was much slimmer in my younger days, mind you. With a nip here, a tuck there, and a good pressing with the iron, this should fit you like a dream.''

Taylor gently pushed the gown aside and gave Ms. Hardigree a spontaneous hug. ''How can I ever thank you?''

Ms. Hardigree sniffed. ''Nonsense!''

Taylor pulled away. ''It isn't nonsense. You've been so good to me, almost like a, well, like a godmother or a guardian or something.''

Ms. Hardigree's eyes twinkled. ''Not as 'hard-nosed' as you thought, eh?''

Taylor turned several shades of red.

Ms. Hardigree chuckled. ''Oh, I'm familiar with the nickname. But don't worry, I like it. Keeps the discipline level up.'' She patted the back of her bun. ''Makes me feel a little notorious, too. Like a woman with a reputation.''

Taylor laughed. ''Ms. Hardigree!''

The administrator caught herself and smiled. ''Now pack that away and hide it in your car before the other volunteers arrive. We wouldn't want it to end up on the auction block with the rest of the old clothes.''

Taylor clutched the package with a horrified expression. ''It's far too special for that.''

Ms. Hardigree made a small clucking sound. ''*You'll* make it special, dear. With any luck, Dr. Frost won't even notice the dress.''

Taylor gave her a puzzled stare, somewhat disappointed. ''You don't think so?''

Ms. Hardigree shook her head. ''He'll notice *you* instead.''

Taylor sighed deeply. ''I hope you're right, Ms. Hardigree, I sincerely hope so.''

The night of the ball, as Taylor spun in front of the mirror, she felt even more hopeful. The dress lay against her skin, soft and radiant, as lustrous as the sheen on a deep sea pearl, the sequins sparkling with mysterious promise in the dim light of her apartment.

''Well, Patches, what do you think?'' she asked the lazy, lounging cat. ''Am I presentable?''

From his resting place on her bed, Patches cocked open one sleepy eye and regarded her with bored indifference. Then he yawned, stretched, and closed it again.

Taylor clipped on a pair of crystal earrings, scolding

softly. ''Some help you are.'' She positioned the gems to her liking, then settled on the bed beside Patches. ''Ms. Hardigree gave me this dress, Patches, but she also gave me something to think about. I've decided I don't want to go through life alone, without someone special to love.''

Patches nudged against her hand, demanding attention.

''Yes, I know I'll always have you, but remember Patches, you *are* just a cat, after all.''

The doorbell rang, denying Patches any opportunity to protest. Taylor rose from the bed, smoothed her gown, and with a final, satisfied glance in the mirror, went to answer the door.

Kayne stood on the threshold, one arm balanced against the jamb. ''Good evening.''

His tuxedo, pressed to scalpel-sharp perfection, outlined every hard, muscled curve of his body with cool, dark precision. The sleek, satin lapels of his jacket and the lean, gleaming stripe on each pant-leg defined the suit with rich, expensive detail. From the toes of his polished leather dress shoes to the black pearl studs nestled in the crisp white pin-tucks of his shirt, Dr. Frost was the picture of sheer masculine beauty.

Gorgeous, Taylor thought, her heart fluttering wildly.

Kayne cut into her thoughts with a low whistle. ''You look gorgeous,'' he commented.

Exactly what I was thinking. ''Thanks,'' she murmured, shutting the door behind him. ''You look— very nice yourself.''

Kayne lifted one dark eyebrow and bowed slightly.

"Your praise overwhelms me. But don't you notice anything different?"

Taylor gave him a puzzled stare. "Different? Like what?"

Kayne turned slowly, inviting her to observe him with greater scrutiny. "You can't tell? It's something I was sure you'd admire."

She scanned his body for a clue. He had the same spice-dark, slightly wavy hair, the same golden-brown tan, the usual gleaming white, faintly mocking smile. He wasn't different, just better than ever. The only difference lay within her. She was hopelessly in love with him.

"Admire?" she whispered hoarsely.

Kayne regarded her warmly, a glint of humor sparkling in his sea-blue eyes. "I can tell you're not exactly following me. Well, let me give you a hint. It's not something I'm wearing, it's something I'm *not* wearing."

Taylor swallowed, more confused than ever.

"Give up?"

She nodded, her mouth dry.

Kayne patted his pockets. "Look, no beeper."

Taylor blinked in surprise. "Of course! You're not wearing your beeper tonight!" She regarded him with suspicious amazement. "What's the catch?"

"No catch. I left a very trusted resident doctor in charge." He tilted her chin back and looked into her eyes. "For this one night at least, we're completely free. No pocket pagers to disturb us. No responsibilities. Just you and me. Together."

Taylor gulped, afraid that he was going to kiss her

here and now. But he didn't. He stood grinning like a naughty schoolboy who'd been caught playing hookey.

"So what's your pleasure, mademoiselle? Dancing 'till dawn? Champagne out of a silver slipper?" His expression softened. "Or a glass one?"

She smiled and glanced down at her feet. No glass slippers there. Just plain-colored pumps purchased on sale. But somehow, it didn't matter. Tonight would be a fairy tale just the same. "Take me to the ball, my prince?" she asked.

Kayne nodded, the teasing gleam still visible in his eyes, and escorted her to the car. He settled her into the passenger seat, then slid into the driver's side, put the car in gear, and took off down the narrow strip of highway.

Kayne pressed a button that opened the car's wide moon-roof, and Taylor looked up to admire the view. The night sky glittered with blue-diamond stars, their pale, pointed rays flickering in and out of the clouds, courting the dark like dancing fireflies. Tiny white Christmas lights dotted the landscape and decked the masts of several sailboats bobbing in the water beyond.

Dr. Frost without a beeper, Taylor mused, gazing at the sky in wonder. A month ago, she wouldn't have thought it possible. But tonight, anything seemed possible.

After all, she had changed too, in the past month. Her understanding of the importance of her work and for the patients had grown, thanks to Kayne's caring involvement. He'd even taught her a few things she hadn't expected to learn. Had Kayne changed as well?

Was he finally willing to make room in his life for a personal relationship?

She stole a glance at him from the corner of her eye. Maybe there was hope for the two of them after all. If Kayne was willing to leave his beeper behind every now and then, if he was willing to compromise, their future looked brighter than ever before. Her mouth curved into a slow, secret smile, and she tipped her head back, enjoying the breeze.

"Happy?" he asked, his eyes still on the road.

"Mmm," she murmured. Very happy. Like a warm, contented cat before a cozy hearth, she felt the sweet satisfaction spreading down to her toes.

He stole a glance in her direction. "Yes, I can see that you are. Let me add a bit of frosting to the cake. I have another piece of news for you."

Taylor turned to watch him. "Yes?"

"It's about the respiratory bears. They've been very beneficial to the patients."

Taylor thought back over the past two weeks of work, to the recovering patients who'd welcomed the bears like old friends. "Even better than I expected," she agreed.

Kayne nodded. "It's been nothing short of remarkable. The patients seem to bond with them. The bears, they're almost empathetic, relieving pain the way they do."

Taylor smiled in understanding, remembering the way the patients had concentrated on the bears rather than on their own discomfort, focusing their attention away from the pain.

"Of course, our findings are preliminary, but I'm

convinced that the bears are actually helping the surgical candidates to recover faster and with less discomfort.''

Taylor held her breath, not daring to hope for what she guessed was coming next.

"At the board meeting," Kayne said, "I'm going to recommend in favor of your 'Bear Care' plan. I'll do everything I can to help you get that extra funding you need."

Taylor let the happiness flow through her. She closed her eyes, basking in sheer delight. He was going to help her! Kayne had put aside his initial skepticism to give her project a chance. The bears had worked their magic.

She leaned over, warm emotion bubbling inside her, and planted a grateful kiss on Kayne's cheek.

He gripped the wheel tighter. "Hey! Watch it now. Are you trying to cause an accident or something?"

Taylor giggled softly. "I'm just so happy. How can I thank you enough?"

He shot her a sidelong glance, rubbing his cheek where she had kissed it. "You're certainly off to a good start." Before she had a chance to respond, Kayne's car phone rang.

He swore softly, hammering his fist on the dashboard. "Oh, no! Not tonight. Couldn't it wait just one night?"

Taylor gave him a worried glance. "Do you know who's calling?"

He nodded grimly. "I know who it is all right. It's the resident I left in charge at the hospital. He had instructions not to call except in case of an extreme emergency.'' He gave Taylor an apologetic frown, his voice mixed with pain and regret. ''Whatever it is, I can guarantee it's not good news.''

The phone rang again, the awful noise shrill and insistent in the darkness.

Kayne shook his head. ''I'm sorry, I have to answer it.''

Taylor swallowed, preparing for the worst. ''Of course.''

Kayne lifted the receiver. ''Tom,'' he said in a calm, even voice. ''What's the problem?''

The question was followed by several minutes of silence as Kayne's face grew increasingly somber. Taylor couldn't hear the voice at the other end of the line. She didn't need to. The tone of the conversation was all too clear. Kayne didn't frown or raise his voice in frustration, but the faint tightening of muscle in his jaw told the whole story. Something was terribly wrong.

He murmured a few curt instructions back to Tom, then replaced the receiver. For a moment, he didn't speak. Taylor waited patiently in agonizing silence.

''What is it?'' she finally whispered when the minutes began to mount and the quiet became suddenly unbearable.

Kayne pulled the car off the road and performed a three-point turn so that it faced the opposite direction. With the engine still running, he took her hand in his. ''Forgive me,'' he said, looking down at her. ''I have to go to the hospital. I can't take you to the ball.''

Taylor took a deep breath, trying hard to contain her disappointment. Whatever it cost her, she could not let the regret show on her face. Kayne didn't need her unhappiness to add to his own frustration. She managed a faint smile. "I understand. By all means, let's go straight to the hospital."

Kayne nodded and pulled the car back onto the highway.

Taylor folded her hands in her lap and stared down at her dress. The sequins caught the light of the stars and threw an eerie, golden glow back at her. She sighed inwardly. So much for her Cinderella-style ball gown. Where was her fairy godmother when she needed her?

She took another deep breath and willed the disappointment away, scolding herself for her selfishness. She was only feeling sorry for herself. At the hospital there was a sick, unfortunate patient whose need was far greater than hers.

"Kayne," she said, as a sudden thought struck her. "Who's the patient?"

He rubbed a hand across his chin, deep in thought. "It's Mitzy Pearl," he said without preamble. "She's been re-admitted."

Taylor squeezed her eyes shut, wincing as if struck by a physical blow. "Oh, Kayne. Not Mitzy. That poor child's been through so much."

Kayne gritted his teeth. "I know. More than any little girl should have to suffer. But it can't be helped. Sometimes, in cases like this, the congenital problem causes a relapse. It's just one of the unknown factors in modern medicine."

Taylor let out a sigh of frustration. "Can you do something to help her?"

Kayne frowned. "I'm not sure at this point. More

than likely she needs a bigger, better equipped hospital to recuperate in. I'll probably recommend transferring her to a larger facility.''

When they pulled into the hospital parking lot, Kayne stepped out of the car and helped Taylor out of the passenger side. He pressed a few bills into her hand. ''Here. Use this to take a cab to the ball.'' He looked down at her with deep regret. ''I'm sure you'll find no lack of willing dance partners.''

She gave the money back to him. ''No way, Dr. Frost. I'm sticking around. Come find me in the waiting lounge when you're through.''

He frowned. ''Are you sure? I don't know how long I'll be.''

Taylor stood her ground. ''Very sure.''

He tapped her gently under the chin. ''Thanks. I will.''

They walked through the double glass entrance doors together and a moment later, Kayne rushed down the hall to the waiting surgical team. Taylor caught a glimpse of Mitzy's parents pacing frantically in the hall, but she turned and walked in the opposite direction to the ladies' restroom. She couldn't begin to explain to them how sorry she felt about Mitzy's relapse. It wouldn't do the couple a bit of good to have her dissolve into a sobbing heap right in front of them. And in another moment, she was sure she'd burst into tears.

It seemed like hours later when Taylor had dried her eyes and settled in for the long, excruciating wait. She'd decided to stretch out on the couch in the waiting room, removing her shoes and arranging the soft satin of her dress as best she could to avoid creasing. She must have fallen asleep, because her next conscious moment occurred a few minutes after midnight, when she heard the sound of footsteps approaching down the hall. The door opened, and Kayne stepped inside.

"I see Cinderella's turned into Sleeping Beauty," he said quietly.

She rubbed her eyes and sat bolt upright on the couch. "How's Mitzy?"

Kayne shook his head gently. "Not good. But we've transferred her to a larger hospital where they've got the kind of staff and equipment she needs. She'll be okay now."

Taylor exhaled slowly. It wasn't good news, but it wasn't bad news either. Stuart General, because of its limited size, was also limited in the amount of sophisticated care they could offer their patients. Kayne had the wisdom to recognize this fact and transfer Mitzy to a more appropriate facility.

In the meantime, he was doing everything he could to upgrade the quality of equipment at Stuart General. In this moment of helpless frustration, Taylor finally understood Kayne's tireless efforts to procure the echocardiogram machine. She began to see the patient care problems from a whole new angle. From *his* side.

Kayne helped her to her feet. "Let's get out of here. Maybe we can still catch the last dance at the ball."

Taylor carefully smoothed her hair and searched the floor for some sign of her shoes.

Kayne let out a low laugh. "Back to Cinderella again. Have you lost your slippers already?"

Taylor grinned at him and bent to retrieve the errant pumps from beneath the couch.

"Come on," he said, taking her by the arm. "I'm no prince, anyway."

Seated in the car again, Taylor mused silently about his comment. No, he wasn't a prince, just a wonderfully caring, ridiculously overworked doctor. Better than a prince, in her opinion.

He turned and surveyed her briefly. "I'm sorry about spoiling your evening, Taylor."

She reached out a hand to touch him. "It wasn't spoiled. We're together now, aren't we?"

He frowned. "Which gives us maybe half an hour out of the entire evening. Not much of a date."

She sighed. "These things happen. It's some kind of unwritten law that applies to the medical profession. It's completely unpredictable."

"Or predictably difficult," Kayne added.

Taylor nodded sagely. "It can be."

He shook his head. "I'm afraid it's the Frost law, the story of my life. Whenever I try to make time for myself, the patients seem to suffer for it."

Taylor stopped him cold. "Mitzy's relapse wasn't your fault. You told me yourself it couldn't be helped. Besides, you were there as soon as you could be."

He didn't look at her, but kept his eyes on the road. "Maybe. Maybe not. But if there's one lesson to be learned from this episode, it's a hard truth to swallow."

Taylor wrinkled her forehead. "What truth is that?"

A muscle tightened in Kayne's jaw. He swallowed hard, lowering his voice to a harsh, broken whisper. "The truth that I've dedicated my life to medicine, and there isn't room for anything else."

''Anything else,'' she repeated softly. ''Meaning me?''

He continued staring straight ahead. ''Forgive me, Taylor. I should never have started something that's not in my power to finish.''

Chapter 8

Taylor turned away from Kayne and stared out into the black night, fighting back the tears that threatened to fall. She would *not* cry in front of him. She simply would not. She started to speak, but the words strangled and died in her throat. There was nothing left to say. Kayne's mind was made up.

He continued driving, keeping his eyes directly on the dark road in front of them. "We're almost to the ball. Will you still come with me?"

Taylor wanted to cry out loud, to insist that he stop the car so she could flee into the darkness, away from the pain. But sheer, obstinate pride kept her from doing any such thing. She spoke, and her own voice sounded strange and far away. "We'd better show up. After all, this year the donations are dedicated for your echo-cardiogram machine." She turned back toward him and answered truthfully, "I wouldn't want to do anything to jeopardize that goal."

Kayne glanced in her direction with surprise, then shot her a look of admiration. "I guess it's my turn to thank you."

Apparently, he expected tears and bitter regret, but

he should've known better. She would *not* agonize over what might have been. Instead she would always be grateful for the precious time they had spent together.

She shook her head vehemently. "It's the least I can do to repay your efforts. You've helped so much with the bears. You've done so much for the children."

He pulled the car up to the posh seaside hotel where the ball was being held, rousing a purple and gold-clad valet from his late-hour boredom. Kayne tossed him the keys. "Park it, please."

The young man eyed the sleek silver Porsche with keen interest. "Nice set of wheels," he commented. "A car phone and everything."

Kayne's brows flickered a little. "Oh, yes, there's definitely a phone, and if you're smart, you'll take the thing off the hook. It never fails to ring at the worst possible moment."

At the valet's puzzled look, Kayne shot back a wry smile and escorted Taylor inside.

She excused herself and headed for the powder room, supposedly to touch up her make-up before entering the main ballroom. What she really needed was a moment alone. She slipped inside the plush-carpeted ladies' lounge, noting with relief that the room was deserted. She settled herself in front of the massive gilt mirror and pretended to comb her hair.

The face staring back at her from the silvered glass looked pale, the eyes too bright and large. She pinched her cheeks lightly, trying to bring some color back into them, but it was no use. The life had drained out of her at Kayne's words. When he'd explained that there was no room for her in his life, he had shattered all of her hopes.

Earlier, when the ringing phone had ruined their evening, Taylor had experienced some disappointment. But she was also able to understand the importance of Kayne's responsibilities. For the first time, she understood the responsibilities that must have weighed on her own father. True, he should have paid more attention to the needs of his wife and child, but she and her mother should have also been more understanding of his work.

Taylor sighed, knowing she'd missed her chance to show Kayne that kind of support and understanding. Just when she'd realized that love required its own kind of sacrifice, Kayne had sacrificed their relationship entirely. For the sake of his work. For the good of his patients.

How could she fight that kind of dedication? She couldn't ask him to compromise for her sake, not if he felt the patients would bear the consequences of that compromise. And she couldn't attempt to convince him otherwise. It wasn't her place. He had to make the decision himself.

Tonight, it seemed he'd made that critical choice once and for all. He'd chosen to live without her. Now, she would simply have to learn to live without him.

The door opened suddenly, admitting Kiki Vandemere into the lounge. Dressed to the nines in a painted-on gown of blood-red silk, the shocking drama of her plunging neckline was offset only slightly by the thigh-high slits that snaked up both sides of the dress. Diamond and ruby clips glittered brilliantly in her shining black hair and winked wickedly at her ears.

"Why, if it isn't Taylor Berne," she said, feigning surprise. "I thought I saw you arrive with Dr. Frost. A little late, aren't you?"

When Taylor only nodded silently, Kiki appraised her with a look of cool disdain. "What an *interesting* dress you're wearing. It appears to be about the same vintage as that bear of yours. What was his name? Mr. Marzipan?"

Taylor tried to come up with an appropriate retort, but she couldn't think of anything bad enough to say. The fight had gone out of her. She averted her gaze from Kiki, and methodically ran the comb through her hair. "Mr. Marmalade," she said tonelessly. "His name's Mr. Marmalade."

"Marzipan, Marmalade, there's not much difference, is there?" Kiki remarked, expertly retouching her lipstick. "The name's so odd I never can seem to remember it." She tried to smile, but her lips merely curved into a thinly-veiled sneer. "You really should think about selling him, sweetie. At least then you'd have enough money to buy a decent dress."

Taylor widened her eyes at the blatant insult, then relaxed her face into a smile. "I haven't seen what everyone else is wearing, Kiki," she said, staring pointedly at the older woman's dress. "But if your outfit is anything to go by, I'd say *indecent* attire is more appropriate." She stood up with what she hoped was calm dignity and left the room, leaving Kiki gaping after her, wide-mouthed.

Kayne was waiting for her in the lobby. She took

his arm and urged him into the ballroom, a high, angry flush on her face. She wanted to escape before Kiki could follow and fling any more poison arrows her way.

As they entered the ballroom, the orchestra leader announced the last dance of the evening, a Christmas waltz. Kayne pulled her onto the dance floor before she could protest, wrapping his arms around her as though he'd never let go. Relinquishing the last remnants of control, Taylor rested her head on his shoulder and prayed for a long waltz. If this was her last dance with Kayne, she never wanted it to end.

A hundred people drifted past them, whirling slowly to the dulcet wail of violins. Bright, jewel-bedecked women floated by, their bow-wrapped gowns fluttering in the arms of elegant, tuxedo-clad men. Potted palm trees twinkled with the glow of golden trim and tinsel.

Too soon, the music ended, the overhead lights turned on and yawning couples began to slowly file out of the ballroom. With the glare of fluorescent lights came the shock of reality. The floor revealed traces of scattered debris—a fallen ribbon from an unwrapped package, the crushed remnants of a fragile Christmas ornament, the butt of a burned-out cigarette. On the stained and wrinkled tablecloths, wilting pine boughs drooped among lipstick-stained glasses and half-finished bottles of wine. The artificial tree in the corner took on a surrealistic glow, its multi-colored lights blinking above the gaudy boxes of pretend presents.

Kayne relinquished his hold on Taylor, but only after several minutes had elapsed. For a moment she thought she had detected a reluctance on his part to let her go.

But the moment was fleeting, and the man who'd held her in his arms too long, long enough to make people stare, quickly regained his professional demeanor, turning back into the cool and clinical Dr. Frost.

He led her to where Ms. Hardigree stood, deep in conversation with Kiki Vandemere. Kayne nodded politely to the two women. "Good evening, ladies."

Taylor eyed Kiki with some trepidation, but she met the woman's malignant glare without flinching. She was immune to it by now. Nothing that Kiki could say or do would hurt her any deeper than she'd already been hurt tonight.

"Merry Christmas, *Kayne*," Kiki breathed, emphasizing his name with intimate familiarity. "Sorry you missed so much of the ball."

Kayne nodded curtly. "There was an emergency at the hospital."

Ms. Hardigree shot Taylor a sympathetic smile. "These things do happen."

Kiki pursed her lips and gave Kayne a speculative stare. "Have you heard the news?"

"The news?" he asked with mild interest. "What is it tonight, Kiki? Something earth-shattering, no doubt. Did the caterers serve the wrong brand of caviar? Or perhaps the wine wasn't exactly at room temperature?"

Kiki simpered back at him with her well-practiced, beauty-queen smile, but it was obvious his words had stung. "Oh, I think you'll find it far more interesting than that. It has something to do with your precious echocardiogram machine."

Kayne's expression sobered. He turned to Ms. Hardigree. "Is there a problem?"

Ms. Hardigree cast an admonishing look in Kiki's direction, then turned to Kayne. "I'm afraid it's very bad news, Dr. Frost, you see—"

"You see," Kiki cut in, "as a fellow board member I feel it's my duty to inform you that tonight's fund-raising efforts weren't as successful as we hoped. It seems the Christmas spirit isn't quite what it used to be. Donations are down this year. We're nearly five thousand dollars short of our goal. It's really too bad, Kayne. It looks like you won't be getting that echocardiogram after all."

White-hot anger flashed through Taylor's heart. She'd thought Kiki's bitterness extended to her alone. She'd thought the woman couldn't hurt her any further. She'd been wrong. Kiki delivered this devastating news with malicious glee, knowing full well the effect it would have on Kayne. Taylor, too, knew the pain he must be feeling at this unexpected blow. She ached for him.

Kayne turned again to Ms. Hardigree, his face drawn and somber. "Is it true?"

Ms. Hardigree nodded miserably. "I'm afraid it is. I don't see how we can raise the extra money. All of our major patrons have already made their pledges."

Kayne drew his brows together, deep in thought. "Maybe if I tried to explain the importance of the machine. . . ."

Ms. Hardigree shook her head. "You already have, by making a generous personal contribution. If the patrons hadn't been so impressed by the amount of your donation, I doubt we would have collected as much as we did. You've done your part, Kayne. We all have. There isn't much more we can do at this point.''

Taylor sighed in frustration. "There must be *something*. What about the auxiliary auction? Won't that raise enough money to put you over the goal?''

Kiki almost sneered. ''The auxiliary auction? You must be joking. That's nothing more than a pitiful sideshow, to keep the do-gooders busy during the holidays. They never sell anything better than cheap, used furniture and worthless, cast-off clothes. They might make a few hundred in a record year, but that won't be nearly enough.''

A choking heaviness settled in Taylor's chest. "So, it's hopeless.''

Kiki curled her thin, painted lips. ''Completely hopeless. Of course, I can understand why you're so disappointed. You realize this means no money for your 'Bear Care' plan either. Not a dime.''

That was something Taylor hadn't considered. Strange, a month ago, it might've been her first concern. But tonight, her initial disappointment was for Kayne's loss, not for her own.

Kayne, apparently, had heard enough. He took Taylor firmly by the hand. ''Let's get out of here.''

He nodded goodnight to Ms. Hardigree and left without a word to Kiki. On their way out, Taylor shot a backward glance at the woman. She was touching up her make-up with the aid of a small hand mirror, reminding Taylor of her favorite childhood fairy tale, in which the wicked queen sought comfort and reassurance in her own, evil beauty.

"She's horrid," Taylor muttered under her breath.

" 'Horrid' is something of an understatement," Kayne added, his jaw clenching in anger.

Taylor smiled grimly. "I'll defer to your diagnosis, Dr. Frost."

Back in the car, on the way to Taylor's apartment, Kayne's voice broke through the gloomy silence. "I wish I'd been there earlier," he confessed into the darkness. "I might've persuaded some of Kiki's society cronies to part with a few extra dollars. It could've made the difference."

Taylor frowned, struggling for the right words. "Don't look back, Kayne. You did what you had to do."

He shrugged his shoulders in mock resignation. "I suppose I tried to do too many things at once. Nothing has worked out quite the way I expected."

She sighed, shriveling at the despair in his voice. "You can't do it all, Kayne. You can't be available one hundred percent of the time. You *are* only human, after all."

He shot her a slow, ironic smile. "Thanks for the compliment, but I think your original opinion of me was closer to the truth. I can't apply normal rules to my life. I can't ask you to sacrifice or settle for anything less than what you deserve."

She took a deep breath, desperation forcing her to admit the truth. "I'm willing to make sacrifices."

He exhaled slowly, clenching and unclenching his fist as if the motion of his hand could give him the strength to speak. ''That's exactly why I can't ask you to.'' He pulled the car into her driveway and, shutting off the motor, took her hand in his. ''You're far too willing, Taylor. Too sweet, too generous, too loving.'' He stopped, and drew a deep, ragged breath. ''I won't take advantage of your generosity.''

She wanted to cry out, to scream that it wasn't generosity that motivated her, but plain and selfish love. She held back her emotions, keeping her voice calm. ''Kayne, please, you don't understand.''

He looked down at her with wise, aqua eyes. ''That's precisely the problem, my dear. I understand far too well.''

With the dark finality of his words, Taylor gave up trying to plead. ''Good night, then,'' she managed, freeing her hand from his and letting herself out of the car.

''Good-bye,'' he said quietly, staring straight ahead.

She let herself into the apartment and drew back the curtains for a last glimpse of Kayne in his shining, silver car. He guided the vehicle down the street, cutting through the darkness like a steel blade slashing into the night.

When Taylor woke the next morning, several minutes passed before full consciousness obliterated her peaceful, sleepy ignorance. When last night's memories finally dawned on her, they brought the aching sadness back, and cold, invisible fingers resumed their painful clutching at her heart.

Patches, sleeping languidly at her feet, awoke with his mistress. He stretched and yawned widely, then sensing that something was wrong, padded across the covers to bestow sandpaper kisses on her cheek.

Taylor took some comfort in his tranquil purring. She reached out to scratch him behind the ears. "Don't worry about me, Patches. I'm going to be just fine."

He settled awkwardly on her chest.

"I'll get over him," she assured him. *By the time I'm ninety or so*, her heart whispered.

Patches pushed his nose against hers.

"In my next life, Patches, I think I'd like to be a cat. Life would be a lot less complicated. I'd find some nice human, someone to love and feed me and I'd get fat and sassy on tuna and cream."

Patches pricked his ears at the sound of those culinary delights.

"And I'd stay away from all the handsome tom cats," she added as an afterthought. "Except you, of course."

Patches tapped her lightly on the face with a gentle, sheathed paw.

"Want your breakfast, eh? Well, I don't know how you can even think of food at a time like this. Besides the abominable mess my love-life is in, there's Mitzy to worry about." She sighed. "I have to admit, Patches, that the bears may not be as special as I thought they were. Things are worse than ever. Even Christmas seems a bit sad this year. Maybe Kiki was right about the lack of spirit."

She scratched Patches behind the ears. "The bears can't help Mitzy now, they can't help Kayne get his echocardiogram—" She stopped suddenly.

Patches felt the tension in her hand and looked up.

"Or maybe they can," she finished quietly. "When I was a child I believed in Mr. Marmalade's magic. Maybe it wasn't such a childish idea after all. Maybe he *is* magic.

"I can't have Kayne's love, Patches. He made that all too clear. But I can still help him, I think. If I could raise the money—" She bit her lip, thinking. "It won't be easy, Patches, in fact it may be the hardest thing I've ever done, but if I sell Mr. Marmalade, it might be enough to put the echocardiogram fund over its goal." She scooted Patches from the bed and stood quickly, throwing on her robe. "I've got to get to the auction. Fast."

With twice her usual speed, Taylor showered, dressed and flew out the door. She was back a moment later, somewhat contrite, remembering she hadn't fed Patches. But as soon as that chore was accomplished, she dashed back out to her car and headed for the hospital.

When she reached the gift shop, Taylor smoothly unlocked the door and let herself in without being spotted. She didn't want to be seen by anyone. A delay of any sort might keep her from accomplishing her goal. She had to reach the auction house in time.

Mr. Marmalade sat patiently on the cart, his wistful shoe-button eyes staring back at her with silent adoration. Taylor's heart sank to her stomach, sudden doubt gripping her soul. This was going to be even harder than she imagined.

She quickly averted her eyes from his face and raised him off the cart into her arms. One last hug, she told herself, cradling the wise old bear against her. "Forgive me," she whispered into his crooked ear, "this is something I *have* to do."

Fighting back the moisture in her eyes, she tucked him securely under one arm and headed out the door.

By the time she reached the auction house, she had regained a measure of control. She loved Mr. Marmalade dearly, but he was really nothing but a remnant of her childhood. Just a stuffed souvenir of her loneliness, a poor substitute for what she'd really wanted all her life—security. The security of love and family.

With calm determination she carried him out of the car and into the crowded auction room. Preparations for the big event were in full swing. Auction volunteers bustled back and forth, checking on last minute details. The contributions had been sorted and tagged and were lined neatly on a long row of display tables. A crowd of potential bidders gathered in front of the displays, inspecting the piles of merchandise.

Taylor searched the room, looking for one person in particular. Ms. Hardigree, knee-deep in a pile of small appliances, waved to her from across the crowds, but Taylor made no attempt to join her. She continued scanning the crowd.

A minute later, she spotted her target. Taylor made her way through the gathering throngs until she was face-to-face with the very person she had come to see. Kiki Vandemere.

At first the woman tried to ignore her, turning away to speak to a volunteer. But Taylor stood her ground. She waited for the volunteer to finish her response, then politely cut in. "Kiki, may I have a word with you, please?"

The volunteer moved away. Kiki shrugged and smoothed the sleeves of her emerald-green designer suit. She looked like a peacock preening its feathers. "You may, but try to make it quick. There are *other* people here I *want* to see."

Taylor didn't miss the implied insult. She gripped Mr. Marmalade a little tighter and continued. "I was wondering if you're still interested in purchasing my Teddy bear."

Kiki glanced down at the furry bundle under Taylor's right arm and a satisfied smirk spread across her meticulously made-up face. "Oh that," she answered, her memory purposely vague. "Mr. Molasses, isn't it?"

Taylor flinched at the name, but she didn't bother to correct it this time. What was the use? If Kiki agreed to purchase the bear, it would be her right to call him anything she wanted.

"I've decided to sell him," Taylor explained, keeping her cool.

Kiki reached out, and without so much as a please or a thank you, wrenched Mr. Marmalade from under Taylor's arm. She held the bear at arm's length, inspecting him as critically as a well-trained jeweler might look upon a sadly flawed gemstone. "He doesn't have fleas, does he?"

"Fleas!" Taylor responded indignantly, "Certainly not. He's in excellent condition for his age," she added.

Kiki tugged at one of Mr. Marmalade's ears, trying

to push it into a more proper position. "That's debatable."

Taylor's expression hardened. "Are you still interested in buying him, or should I ask someone else?"

Kiki gave her a cool, appraising look. "Don't be so hasty. I'm still interested. As long as the price is right."

Taylor breathed a sigh of relief and named a reasonable price. Considering the age and rarity of the bear, the price was on the low side, but she didn't intend to be greedy, and the money would be enough to meet the goal. "It's for a good cause," she added. "I'm donating the money to the hospital, for Kayne's echocardiogram machine."

Kiki narrowed her eyes, sneering sarcastically, "How noble of you."

Taylor ignored the insult. She didn't care how condescending the woman was, as long as she came through with the money.

"I'll give you half," Kiki said, plucking at the remaining threads on Mr. Marmalade's nose with her sharp, polished fingernails. "He's in dreadful condition."

"Half?" Taylor asked, incredulous. "You can't be serious. He's not perfect, but he's certainly worth every penny I'm asking for." Besides, she reasoned silently, half the asking price would not be enough to put the echocardiogram fund over its goal.

Kiki held Mr. Marmalade closer to her slightly turned-up nose and sniffed. "And he smells dreadful— musty, like old books or something."

Taylor exhaled slowly, fighting for control. "He's

almost an antique, Kiki, what did you expect? Besides, some people actually *like* the smell of old books.''

"Well, I'm not one of them. This bear needs a thorough fumigating, his paws need replacing and he needs a new set of eyes.'' Kiki rubbed her thumbs across Mr. Marmalade's sweet, shoe-button eyes. "They look so—old.''

Taylor nearly cringed at the thought of Mr. Marmalade with so many new body parts. He wouldn't be the same at all. Half the charm of older Teddies lay in their not-so-perfect, well-loved faces. She couldn't begin to imagine Mr. Marmalade with a new expression.

"Kiki," Taylor said slowly, trying to approach the problem from an angle that would appeal to Kiki most, "if you attempt to restore him to brand-new condition, you'll ruin his value. Many collectors appreciate the 'played with' look of old bears.''

Kiki lowered her voice to a near hiss. "I didn't ask for your opinion, did I, Miss Berne? My offer still stands. Take it or leave it.''

Taylor shook her head in wonder. "Doesn't the echocardiogram fund mean anything to you? Think of the patients it could help, think of—''

"It's half or nothing," Kiki interrupted, smiling at the desperation in Taylor's voice. "Do I make myself clear?''

Very clear, Taylor admitted unhappily. It was all too clear that the woman couldn't care less about the echocardiogram. The only thing Kiki cared about was herself.

Okay, Taylor, she told herself silently. You've got two choices. Take what she offers and hope to make the money up somewhere else or . . .

She reached out and snatched Mr. Marmalade back from Kiki's grasp. "Thanks, but I'll find another buyer."

Kiki tried to appear unconcerned. "Do whatever you like, but you'll come crawling back to me sooner or later. You'll never find another buyer willing to spend that kind of money." She pursed her lacquered lips into a smug smile. "At least, you won't find one in time."

Taylor lifted her chin with cool defiance. "We'll see about that." With a confident stride she didn't really feel, she turned and walked away.

Now what? she wondered in desperation. She'd enjoyed standing up to Kiki, although she hadn't said half of what she'd wanted to. Sheer desperation had kept most of the choice remarks from leaving the tip of her tongue. Kiki was still a member of the hospital board, and although Taylor's "Bear Care" plan looked hopeless for the present, she didn't want to ruin the chance of Kiki's support for future projects. Too many children depended on it.

But she still had to find a buyer for Mr. Marmalade and she had to find one *now*. Taylor sank into a nearby chair, one of many that had been set up for the auction. She balanced Mr. Marmalade on her lap and stared into his funny old face, hoping for inspiration.

Resting her chin on his head, she stared absently at the piles of cast-off merchandise that lined the tables.

Plastic holly branches, broken toys and past-season clothes. If only there was something of value in all that stuff.

She caught her breath and took another look at Mr. Marmalade. "Of course," she said. "It couldn't be simpler."

Ms. Hardigree finally made her way over to Taylor's chair. "I see you've brought Mr. Marmalade along," she said, smiling down at them. "Is he going to watch the auction with you?"

Taylor shook her head thoughtfully. "With your help, Ms. Hardigree, he's going to be *in* the auction."

Ms. Hardigree's jaw dropped. "You're going to donate him? But isn't he a family heirloom?"

Taylor nodded. "He is, but please don't try to talk me out of it. I've already made up my mind. Kiki won't pay me what he's really worth. Do you think there's still time to tag him and put him up for sale?"

Ms. Hardigree scratched her chin. "Putting him in the auction shouldn't be a problem, dear, but, well, I feel I have to warn you, he might not sell for the price you want. Oh, I don't doubt he's worth a great deal, but in an auction, you never know. He may not even sell for as much as Kiki's willing to pay."

If Mr. Marmalade only sold for a few dollars, at least she would have given it her best shot. Maybe this time, fate would be on her side. "I understand," Taylor said, swallowing hard. "But I have to try."

Chapter 9

The auctioneer finally took his place behind the podium and hammered his gavel with brisk authority. An expectant hush fell over the assembled crowd. They held their numbered bidding paddles poised, ready for the excitement to begin. Mr. Marmalade sat, as haphazardly as any other cast-off item, among the tangled cords of used appliances, beneath the garish, fringed shade of an over-gilded lamp.

From her seat in the back row, Taylor shot a nervous glance to the chair beside her. "Ms. Hardigree," she whispered, "how long before his number's called?"

Ms. Hardigree shrugged, rolling an old lace hankie in her hands with restless agitation. "It's hard to say, since he was one of the last items to be added. I expect we'll have quite a wait." She unrolled the hankie, then started to twist it again in the opposite direction. "I don't know how you can be so calm, Taylor. I'm a nervous wreck already, and the auction's only just starting." She lifted her head to assess the crowd. "Look at all those empty seats," she muttered in some disgust. "The turn-out doesn't appear to be very good this year."

Taylor's heart sank at this dismal pronouncement, but she wouldn't give up hope so fast. She had to believe in Mr. Marmalade. "It only takes two interested bidders to bring a good price. Surely there are two people in this crowd who might be interested in a fine, collectible bear."

Ms. Hardigree threaded the handkerchief through her fast-working fingers. "I hope you're right, but I do wish that auctioneer would hurry up. He's only on item four! At this rate, we'll be here 'till July!"

Taylor sighed heavily and settled back in her chair to wait. Indeed the auctioneer was not the free-wheeling, fast-talking type. Every word he uttered was painfully slow, perfectly clear, and pronounced in a maddeningly lazy southern drawl. He definitely wasn't going to win any awards for speed. Nor did he seem capable of whipping the crowd into a buying frenzy.

Taylor fought the growing dread in her stomach, the hard, cold lump that had settled deep in her belly. She began to wonder if she'd made a terrible, irrevocable mistake. What if Mr. Marmalade sold for less than Kiki had offered? What if she'd sacrificed him for nothing?

She turned to Ms. Hardigree, choking back the panic in her voice. "What have I done?"

Ms. Hardigree made a brisk, clucking sound. "Don't fret, Taylor. It's like this every year."

Taylor frowned. "Surely the auction would do better if they tried to find a more professional auctioneer?"

Ms. Hardigree shook her head. "The committee's tried, but they haven't been able to fire this one. Kiki won't hear of it. He's related to her family. A second cousin once-removed or some such thing.''

Taylor hung her head in frustration. ''I might've guessed. No wonder they never make any money. I don't think that man could make a free cruise around the world sound exciting, not to mention a beat-up, balding bear.''

Ms. Hardigree nodded apologetically. ''One year he actually sold a woman's hat right off her head! It wasn't supposed to be in the auction, of course, but she was sitting in the front row and, well, the auctioneer's eyesight isn't what it used to be. I think he mistook it for a silk flower arrangement.''

The lump in Taylor's stomach grew to the size of a basketball. ''I don't feel very well.''

Ms. Hardigree handed her the handkerchief. ''Take this, dear, and wipe your forehead. You can't be sick now. I think Mr. Marmalade may be coming up next.''

Taylor took several deep swallows of air and watched with detached fascination as the slow-moving auctioneer finally lifted Mr. Marmalade from the table and held him high for the inspection of the crowd. A low buzz of interest rose from the audience. Taylor leaned forward, her expectations bolstered by this positive sign. But a minute later, her hopes were dashed again.

When the auctioneer announced the opening bid of a thousand dollars, the crowd groaned in disappointment. They hadn't expected the price to start so high. The awful silence that followed seemed to last for hours. The auctioneer stood blinking at the podium, waiting expectantly for a bid. Taylor's stomach began to churn.

No one spoke.

"Come on, folks," the auctioneer finally prompted after several agonizing minutes. "Won't somebody make a bid for this fine Teddy bear?"

Silence prevailed again. There were still no bidders. After another excruciating minute, Taylor couldn't stand it any longer. Mechanically, she rose from her chair, propelled by an invisible power within her. She walked to the front of the room and stood resolutely before the curious crowd. The auctioneer stared at her, dumbfounded, then recovering from his momentary surprise, he relinquished the podium and stepped aside to let her speak.

Taylor ran her hand across Mr. Marmalade's fur, gaining strength from his touch. Now, more than ever, she needed his magical inspiration. She bent her head to the microphone, her courage bolstered by the just-ness of her cause and the sheer conviction in her heart.

"This bear," she said in a soft, confident voice, "is very old. In fact, he's almost an antique." She swallowed hard, and gave Mr. Marmalade a loving tap on the head. "That alone is a good reason to buy him."

She paused thoughtfully, gazing fondly at the bear, and continued: "He will probably increase in value over the coming years—another good reason to buy him." She lifted her chin and sent a challenging look across the room. "But I've got a better reason. A very simple one. Our hospital needs your support."

A positive murmur rising from the audience urged her to continue. "Last night," she said, fighting back the lump in her throat, "a sick little girl had to leave our hospital for a bigger, better equipped facility. Stuart

General couldn't help her.'' She tightened her grip on the podium and continued. ''Many of you know me as 'Doc' Berne. Well, I'm just a Teddy bear doctor, not a real one, but I do see the need for more hospital equipment.''

''*Please*,'' she said, the emotion strong in her voice, ''we're very close to our goal of obtaining a new echocardiogram machine. If a few of you would only open up your hearts,'' she hesitated, smiling, ''and your pocketbooks—we could reach that goal—together.''

With a final pat for Mr. Marmalade, she relinquished her place at the podium and walked quickly back to her seat.

The auctioneer stepped back into place. ''Well,'' he drawled in a voice as slow as ever, ''that was certainly an inspiring speech. Very inspiring. Now, I'll give it one more try, to see if any of you were paying attention to the little lady. What's my opening bid for this fine Teddy bear?''

Taylor held her breath, waiting, hoping that somebody had been listening. For a moment it seemed as though no one had heard. Then an over-dressed woman in the front row, with a pale, powder-caked face and wild, unruly red hair, raised her paddle. ''One thousand dollars!'' she called out.

Taylor exhaled slowly, relief flooding through her. She craned her neck for a better view of the bidder, but another movement caught her eye. Kiki Vandemere shifted uncomfortably in her seat.

''You've done it!'' Ms. Hardigree exclaimed. ''Taylor, I think your speech worked! You've actually done it!''

Taylor bit her lip as the bidding slowly escalated. It wasn't over yet. "Who is that?" she whispered, indicating the red-haired woman who was bidding.

"Don't you know?" Ms. Hardigree responded, a wicked gleam in her eyes. "That's Kiki's arch-rival, old Mrs. Puffenhall. She's rich as Croesus—lives in a spooky old house full of antiques. Her favorite pastime is terrorizing the neighborhood children at Halloween."

Taylor gave her a puzzled look. "So why is she Kiki's rival?"

Ms. Hardigree grinned. "Puffenhall is the only one in town with a better antique collection than Kiki's. Those two have been trying to out-buy each other for years. Just like two greedy weasels at an egg banquet."

Taylor couldn't help smiling at Ms. Hardigree's words. The growing bids raised her spirits higher still. Mrs. Puffenhall's price of three thousand dollars was already more than Kiki had offered to pay.

Then a man in the middle row called out "Thirty–one hundred!" sending the price and Taylor's hope soaring. When Puffenhall upped the ante to thirty–five hundred, the man simply shrugged his shoulders and lowered his paddle, the amount apparently beyond his means.

Just as the auctioneer was about to hammer down the final bid, Kiki raised her paddle and grudgingly said, "Thirty–six hundred."

"I knew it!" Ms. Hardigree exclaimed. "Kiki won't give up a prize like that to Puffenhall."

Taylor's eyes widened in astonishment. "How high do you think she's willing to go?"

Ms. Hardigree shook her head in mischievous delight. "Who knows? But at least this time, the hospital will benefit from all that greed."

Puffenhall raised her paddle again, driving the price over four thousand.

Ms. Hardigree snorted. "Poor Kiki. She'll have to mortgage the mansion to afford this one."

When Kiki outbid the woman again, rashly raising the amount to forty–five hundred, Taylor's jaw dropped. An hour ago, Kiki hadn't been so eager to part with her money. At the first sign of competition, she was ready to spend it all.

When the price hit five thousand, Taylor's face relaxed into a comfortable smile and she sat back to enjoy the final showdown. Back and forth the bidding went, first to Kiki, then to Mrs. Puffenhall, then back again to Kiki. The crowd held its collective breath waiting for a winner. When the war was finally over, and the auctioneer hammered down the final price of ten thousand dollars, Mrs. Puffenhall stormed off in an angry huff and Kiki emerged the victor. Sort of.

Winning the battle had cost her dearly. She'd have to give up a great many manicures to afford her new treasure. But at the moment, she seemed determined to make the most of her triumph. She approached Taylor with flashing eyes, dangling Mr. Marmalade from one heavily jeweled hand.

"He's finally mine," she said coldly. "A Christmas present to myself. Let that be a lesson to you, Taylor Berne. I always get what I want." Her lips thinned to a faint smile. "But I'm a gracious winner. I thought I'd give you an opportunity to kiss your little Teddy bear good-bye—forever."

Taylor ignored the bitter comment and managed to smile sweetly. "Why, thank you, Kiki." She bent and dropped a playful peck on Mr. Marmalade's nose. "Good job, old bear." She turned and left the room before Kiki had a chance to respond.

Outside, Ms. Hardigree thanked her profusely for the donation. "It was so generous, Taylor," she insisted. "So like you. The entire hospital owes you a debt of gratitude. Dr. Frost will be especially pleased."

Taylor shook her head vehemently. "Please don't tell him. I—I wouldn't want him to think I did it for the wrong reasons."

Ms. Hardigree frowned, dissatisfaction evident in her stern gaze. "He's going to find out sooner or later. It was his personal contribution that started the drive in the first place. If it wasn't for Dr. Frost's generosity, this hospital couldn't begin to afford that echocardiogram. He'll want to know where this final donation came from."

Taylor shook her head again. "I know I can count on you not to say anything."

Ms. Hardigree gave her a non-committal smile. "I doubt you'll keep it a secret for long. Pretty soon everyone's going to hear how Mr. Marmalade saved the day. They'll have to admit I was right about you and those bears all along. You *are* magic."

Taylor looked away, wistful. "Mr. Marmalade was, anyway."

After she said good-bye to Ms. Hardigree, Taylor headed for home, replaying the morning's events in her mind. She was proud that she'd been able to take Kiki's cruelty in stride and had even managed not to cry. It hadn't been easy, but the experience had taught her a valuable lesson.

As a child, she'd endowed Mr. Marmalade with many wonderful qualities—understanding, wisdom, love, even magic. Today she'd learned that her Teddy bear was just an aging stuffed animal, after all. Just a worn scrap of fabric for a body, a dark skein of thread for a nose, a pair of scuffed shoe-buttons for eyes.

She still believed in the magic. But now she realized that it existed, not in the fur and stuffing, not in the bears themselves, but rather in the love that people projected onto them. *That* was magic.

The following week, many people who'd attended the auction stopped by the gift shop to see Taylor. Did she have other Teddy bears available for sale? Something more affordable than Mr. Marmalade, perhaps? A new Teddy that could become their own heirloom?

Happily adopted bears of all colors, shapes, and sizes walked out the door in record numbers. The holiday season boosted sales even further and come Christmas on Saturday, Taylor knew the bears would help spread the spirit of the season. By the end of the week, nearly everyone in town had passed through her door; everyone, that is, except Kayne Frost.

As busy as ever, he kept up his grueling schedule, sparing no time to stop and talk. Taylor tried to convince herself that it was for the best, that it really didn't matter—there was nothing left to say between them anyway. But his cool professionalism hurt her now more than ever.

Kayne himself appeared to be suffering from the

effects of his self-imposed schedule. When she saw him in the hall once, surrounded by his operating team, she noted the quick vitality had gone out of his step; the spark of intensity was missing from his eyes. She knew that he was experiencing his own form of pain, knew it as surely as she knew her own heart, but it was unclear whether the cause was simple overwork or self-recrimination over Mitzy's relapse.

How long, she wondered, would she be able to face those chance encounters without giving her own feelings away? How long could she remain at Stuart General?

In an attempt to deny the painful truth and refrain from any further speculation about the future, she tried to keep her mind on business and the upcoming meeting of the hospital board.

Even though no funds could currently be spared for her ''Bear Care'' plan, she still planned to attend the meeting. More money would be available in future years, and with a little persuasion on her part, perhaps some of it could be allocated for bear therapy.

Christmas day was particularly painful for Taylor, because she'd elected to spend it alone. Despite invitations from both her father and Nita, Taylor resolved to let each family enjoy their happiness without her. She wouldn't let her miserable mood spoil everyone else's joy. Patches was the only one truly pleased with this decision, and the two of them spent the day crying and purring.

On Monday morning, Taylor had regained her determination, and she paced outside the boardroom, waiting her turn to be called. The giant moths that flapped inside her stomach were not beating their wings in fear of facing the board. She was well-prepared for that—confident even. The anxiety was caused by a completely different fear—the fear of seeing Kayne face-to-face for the first time in a week.

The wide door to the boardroom creaked open and Ms. Hardigree poked her head into the hall. "We're ready for you now, Taylor." She lowered her voice and winked encouragingly. "Go get 'em, girl."

Taylor winked back, with a bravado she didn't quite feel, then followed Ms. Hardigree inside.

The board members sat around a long mahogany table, uncomfortably poised in stiff banker's chairs, their expressions stern and forbidding. Most of the faces were only vaguely familiar to Taylor, but two she recognized instantly.

Kiki was there, immaculately dressed in a stunning gray suit, with luminous black pearls dripping from her ears and coiling in long, snake-like strands about her throat. Kayne sat next to her, the picture of cool propriety in his starched white lab coat. Only his deep-water eyes betrayed the complexity of the man underneath.

Those piercing blue eyes followed her every move with an all-consuming intensity. For the first time in a week, Taylor was grateful for the presence of other people, thankful not to be facing him alone.

She slipped into her designated seat, and the chairman of the board addressed her. "Miss Berne, we've just heard a remarkable report from Dr. Frost regarding your bear therapy. I think we're all in agreement here that funds should be made available to further your efforts.'' He paused significantly as a murmured assent from the other members spread around the room.

Taylor shot a quick, questioning look in Kayne's direction, hoping for a hint of what he'd told them, but his cool, businesslike expression revealed nothing. It was obvious from the board's unanimous approval that he'd taken up the cause himself, sparing her the trouble. For that small favor, she was truly grateful. She wasn't sure she had it in her to make yet another impassioned plea. Lately, the passion had simply gone out of her.

''Unfortunately,'' the chairman continued, ''there is no money available at this time.''

Taylor nodded silently. No surprises there.

The chairman droned on. ''Perhaps during our next fiscal year, the budget can be adjusted to allocate a fair percentage of the liquid assets towards the achievement of that end, satisfying not only the strong interest of our anonymous supporters and relegating . . . ''

Taylor lost track of his speech somewhere along the way, unable to focus on anything but Kayne's presence. He sat only a few feet away, his body relaxed with its usual, easy grace. One restless hand tapped a pen impatiently against the desk and a dark wave of hair fell rakishly over his eye.

Taylor took a precious minute to study him. She memorized every line of his body and savored every angle of his face. Soon, the memories would be all she had left of him. The moment she'd walked into the room, the moment she'd seen his face again, she'd known there was only one solution to her problem. She had to leave Stuart General—and Kayne—forever.

"In short, Miss Berne, the board has called you here to thank you. Ms. Hardigree explained how your generous donation to our auction saved the day. The echocardiogram has been ordered, and thanks to you, can be paid for in full. We owe you our sincere and heartfelt gratitude."

Taylor shot Ms. Hardigree an admonishing look, but it was hard to be angry with someone for lavishing praise upon you. "I was happy to help," she answered quietly.

Rousing herself from a state of obvious boredom, Kiki straightened in her chair and narrowed her eyes at Taylor. "I'm sure we all appreciate Miss Berne's little sacrifice. *I*, for one, have been after her for months to part with that bear, and I'm glad she finally saw the wisdom of my advice. You see, I knew it was a very valuable item, and I was only glad to be of further service to this hospital. I know that you appreciate all of *my* efforts, as well, especially my generous donation. It just proves that I would do anything to support Stuart General."

Several of the board members shifted restlessly in their seats, either confused or embarrassed by Kiki's declaration. Even Kayne stiffened in his chair and leveled a sharp, freezing gaze at Kiki, a look so cold and scornful that it made Taylor feel almost sorry for the woman.

Only Ms. Hardigree didn't seem to be bothered by Kiki's self-congratulatory speech. She clapped politely, urging the other board members to follow suit. "Why, thank you, Kiki. Everyone, could we please show our support for Miss Vandemere? You see, Kiki has generously agreed to donate that wonderful bear back to the hospital!''

Everyone looked at Kiki in shocked surprise. Kiki herself looked fairly flabbergasted. Her jaw dropped, and she gave Ms. Hardigree a blank stare.

''That's right,'' Ms. Hardigree continued, apparently oblivious to the uncomprehending expression on Kiki's face. ''We have plans to set up a permanent display of old bears in our hospital. A display that all the patients will be able to enjoy. Since Kiki is the first to contribute a bear to this worthy project, Mr. Marmalade will always have a place of honor in the display.''

Kiki had recovered from the shock sufficiently to attempt speech, but when she opened her mouth to protest, Ms. Hardigree cut in quickly. ''Remember, Kiki, you said you'd do *anything* for Stuart General.'' Then Ms. Hardigree led the group in another round of applause.

In the face of this enthusiastic response, Kiki clamped her lips shut tightly, realizing she'd been out-maneuvered. She plastered a benevolent smile across her face and tried to appear gracious. The effect was like a female grizzly who'd gone in search of honey and ended up with a mouth full of bees.

Taylor couldn't suppress a grin of her own and shot Ms. Hardigree a warm look filled with gratitude. Ms. Hardigree returned it with a slow, knowing wink, then turned back to the board, the very picture of innocence. ''Shall we call this meeting adjourned?''

When the members began filing into the hall, Kayne was cornered by an older woman with blue-white hair, and Taylor managed to escape without speaking to him.

She followed Ms. Hardigree back to her office, anxious to complete the painful chore ahead of her.

Ms. Hardigree shut the door behind them and motioned Taylor into a seat. "Something tells me we'd better both be sitting down for this one." She sank her ample frame into the executive cushions. "If you're here to tender your resignation, Taylor, please don't bother. I won't accept it."

Taylor's eyes widened in surprise. "How did you know?"

Ms. Hardigree frowned back at her. "I suspected it the minute I saw you lay eyes on Dr. Frost this morning. I can guess the reason. It's written all over your face."

Taylor self-consciously raised her hands to her cheeks. "Is it that obvious?"

Ms. Hardigree smiled gently. "To most people, no, it isn't. But remember, I had a broken heart once, too."

Taylor groaned inwardly at the term "broken heart", but she couldn't think of a more accurate description for the chronic, aching pain within her. The description fit. Her heart was shattered.

"I'm fine," she lied.

"Of course you are," Ms. Hardigree said matter-of-factly. "Even though you don't really believe it right now, you will be fine, eventually. But you won't ever be the same again, either."

Taylor nodded silently. The words were all too true, too accurate, to deny.

Ms. Hardigree leaned forward. "It's still my job to keep good employees, Taylor. I don't want this hospital to lose you. But I do understand what you're going through. I'm making arrangements to put volunteers in charge of the gift shop. I want you to take a couple of weeks off. Goodness knows, you've earned it. Then come back and we'll decide what to do.''

Taylor sighed heavily, remembering another encounter in this same office, many weeks ago. She and Frost had been incompatible then, the differences between them seemingly insurmountable. Nothing had really changed. They were just as incompatible now. As unsuitable for each other as oil and water. The relationship had been doomed from the start.

A week off, or a month, or even a year wouldn't make any difference. It wouldn't change the situation. It wouldn't change the way she felt. She would still have to leave Stuart General, and Kayne, behind. But a few days might give Ms. Hardigree time to adjust to her resignation. Taylor owed her that much. ''Okay, if you think that's best,'' she agreed, rising from her chair.

She stopped on her way out the door and turned back, smiling. ''By the way, I can't think of a better way for Mr. Marmalade to spend his later years.''

Ms. Hardigree sniffed and pretended to examine the papers on her desk. ''With the right—er—inspiration, Kiki can be very generous.''

Taylor smiled faintly. ''Ms. Hardigree, you're one of the most inspiring women I've ever met. Thank you.''

Ms. Hardigree waved her away. ''Nonsense!''

Taylor made a quiet exit, shutting the door behind her.

She stopped by the gift shop briefly, and after noting that a cheerful volunteer was already assisting the customers, Taylor made her way out to her car. Before she could manage to unlock the door, someone removed the keys from her hand.

"Did you think you could slip away without talking to me?" Kayne asked, his voice lethal-soft.

She took a quick breath, her heart pounding. "No, I—I didn't think there was anything to talk about."

He let out an exasperated sigh, running his fingers roughly through his hair. "What about the auction? You weren't even going to tell me about that?"

She looked away, unable to face those dark, unfathomable eyes.

His hands gripped her shoulders. "Look at me, Taylor! Weren't you even going to let me thank you?"

She searched his face, trying to identify the emotion written there. "It wasn't necessary," she answered softly.

He tightened his grip on her arms, struggling to keep his frustration in check. "Look, I know it isn't necessary, but I wanted to tell you I understand the sacrifice you made. I wanted to tell you—"

She held her breath, waiting. "Yes?"

He released her carefully, regaining a measure of composure. "I wanted to tell you I was wrong about the bears—about a lot of things. I have to admit there *is* something special about those Teddy bears, and something very special about you. Something that defies all my scientific principles."

She shook her head slowly. "I think I'm the one who was wrong. I applied those useful scientific methods of yours and made a few discoveries of my own. I learned that the bears are only fluff and stuffing after all—the magic comes from within."

He studied her face. "I think I know how much Mr.

Marmalade meant to you. Why did you do it, Taylor? Why did you give him up?''

She closed her eyes briefly. ''Don't make me answer that, Kayne. It's very complicated. I'm not sure I know all the reasons myself.''

''I know you did it for the hospital, to help the patients, but I think—I hope there was more to it than that.'' He drew her into his arms, and the smoldering eyes that looked down into hers were heavy with unspoken emotion. ''Tell me the other reason, Taylor.''

She swallowed convulsively, reeling from the sapphire blue persuasion in his eyes. She parted her lips to speak, but a sudden, startling noise cut her answer short. Kayne's beeper.

Sighing, he let her go and switched the pocket pager off. ''Sorry,'' he said, an apologetic look on his face. ''I was expecting that, but not quite so soon.'' He spread his hands wide. ''Look, I've got to go.''

He turned back toward the hospital, then suddenly remembering something, tossed her keys back to her. ''Next time,'' he said, ''you won't get off so easily.''

After he'd disappeared into the building, Taylor retreated to the safety of her car, and tried to calm herself for the drive home. With any luck, she promised herself, there wouldn't be a ''next time''. She would be gone from Stuart General.

Chapter 10

Two days later, Taylor decided what to do. She would take the two weeks off that Ms. Hardigree had suggested and visit her father in Ft. Lauderdale. He'd given her an open invitation to "come and visit anytime." Well, now was as good a time as any.

And when the two weeks were over? Well, she'd still have to leave for good. She'd still have to call Ms. Hardigree and tender her resignation. A week or two away wouldn't change anything. It would still hurt too much to stay at Stuart General.

With a sad heart, she made the final preparations for her trip. Her neighbor had agreed to stop by once a day to feed Patches. The mailman had promised to hold her mail. There wasn't much left to do but pack.

Nita's kids, who had come over for a good-bye visit, were giving plenty of help in that department. Taylor had wanted a chance to tell them herself that she was leaving. This time, she tried to explain, she was only going to be gone for two weeks. But later, she would be going away for good.

Josh crawled onto Taylor's bed, balancing precariously on the springy mattress, and tried to climb into her suitcase. "Take me with you," he pleaded.

Taylor lifted him gently into her lap and struggled for an explanation that his three-year old brain would understand. "It wouldn't be any fun for you, Josh. I'm going away for a long time. Pretty soon, you'd be ready to come back home. You'd miss your Mommy."

Katie paused in her exploration of Taylor's makeup case to offer a few sage words of advice. "She's right, Josh. You'd probably bawl your eyes out the first night, anyway."

Lily nodded solemnly. "I feel like bawling myself, and I'm not even as little as Josh."

So do I, Taylor added silently. She gave Josh a big bear hug, unwilling to let go until his chubby, buddha-body squirmed impatiently for release. "Why don't we try to think of something happier?" she suggested.

Josh scrambled back onto the floor and tried to corner Patches under the bed. Lily pushed her hands in the pocket of her jeans and shot Taylor a skeptical stare. Katie, with a diplomacy worthy of a goodwill ambassador, resumed her role as speaker for the group. "Like what?" she asked.

"Like chocolate ice cream?" Taylor suggested, folding a cotton sweater into the suitcase and trying to smile.

Josh's ears perked up at her words, giving Patches ample opportunity for escape. "Ice cream!" he said, clapping his hands together.

"Are we going to the deli?" Katie asked.

"Not exactly," Taylor told her, zipping up the luggage with a firm, if somewhat reluctant, hand. "I just happen to have a gallon of Crunchy Chunky Chocolate right here in my freezer. I thought we'd have a going-away party, just the four of us. What do you say?''

The girls nodded and followed her into the kitchen for the planned festivities, but the general lack of enthusiasm in their response didn't help to brighten the rainy afternoon. Even little Josh seemed to sense the dismal mood. The children were as gloomy as the weather but not half as gloomy as Taylor felt.

When Nita finally came to pick the kids up, Taylor realized her farewell party idea had been a foolish one. Parties were for happy occasions, not for good-byes.

''Good grief, what's wrong with this crew?'' Nita asked after two minutes in the apartment. ''You all look like a pack of ants at a sugar-free picnic. What's the matter?''

The children abandoned their half-finished bowls of ice cream for the safety of their mother's arms. ''We don't want her to go, Mom. Don't let Taylor go.''

Taylor sent an apologetic glance over their heads to Nita. ''Sorry. I guess I didn't do much to cheer them up.''

Nita dug some tissues from her purse and passed them out to the kids. ''Good thing I showed up when I did. A few minutes later and there'd be nothing left of this bunch but a giant sobbing heap!'' The children giggled at the silly, soggy description and settled back in their seats at the kitchen table.

''As for you,'' Nita said, shaking her finger at Taylor. ''I'm still not finished with you. Are you sure you want to do this? Are you really going to go away and leave us all?''

Taylor grabbed a spare tissue from Nita's hand and lightly dabbed her own eyes. "My mind's made up. Don't you see, Nita? I have to go."

Nita shook her head. "No, I'm afraid I don't see. Furthermore, I don't understand why Kayne Frost is willing to let you go. Some brilliant physician he is. He ought to stop working long enough to have his own head examined."

Taylor sniffed, tearing at the tissue. "It's not his fault," she said, loyalty prompting her defense. "He doesn't know I'm leaving."

Nita's dark eyes widened dramatically. "You haven't told him? Taylor, how could you? The man at least deserves to know you're leaving and where you're going." She stopped, wrinkling her forehead. "Are you still planning to see your father?"

Taylor nodded, smiling through the tears. "At least one good thing's come out of this whole mess. I've made peace with my dad. I'm finally beginning to understand the strain he was under as a busy doctor. I thought I'd go visit him for a while, renew our acquaintance, so to speak. After that," she shrugged, "who knows? Maybe I'll find a job in a museum somewhere. I've gotten pretty good at restoring old bears. Maybe I can get a job in textile restoration."

Nita shook her head, frowning. "And bury yourself away for the next thirty years like some dusty old relic? I don't like it, Taylor. Not one bit."

Luckily, the phone rang, sparing Taylor from further argument. She picked up the receiver in record time, avoiding Nita's scowling stare. "Oh, hello, Ms. Hardigree."

"Thank goodness I caught you at home, Taylor," the administrator responded in apparent relief. "I've got some news for you that simply won't wait."

Taylor bit her lower lip, wondering if Ms. Hardigree had dreamed up some new tactic to keep her at Stuart General. She appreciated the woman's loyalty, but longed to convince her once and for all that she still intended to resign. Her mind was made up. No new information, no matter how earth-shattering, could make her change it.

"Yes?" Taylor prompted, moderately curious.

"Would you rather have the good news first, or the bad?"

Taylor groaned inwardly. At this moment, she didn't think she could stand any more bad news. "The good news, first, Ms. Hardigree, by all means."

"Yes, dear, well, the good news is that I didn't tell him you'd resigned."

Taylor frowned. "Tell who, Ms. Hardigree?"

"Why, Kayne, of course. You'll be glad to know I didn't let it slip."

Taylor paused, barely able to ask, "You spoke to Kayne?"

Ms. Hardigree's voice lowered an octave. "I'm afraid I did. It couldn't be helped, Taylor. He came to see me . . ."

Taylor could feel the older woman's hesitation. Her apprehension crept through the line like a foreboding phantom, invisible, yet cold and palpable. "Go on," Taylor said, gripping the phone.

Ms. Hardigree's tone grew apologetic. "Which brings us to the bad news. I'm truly sorry, Taylor, but

I had no choice—I told him you were leaving for two weeks."

Taylor's stomach grew queasy. She shifted uneasily in her chair. "You did?"

She fought back an almost irresistible urge to ask for further details. What did it matter how Kayne had reacted to the news? She had to quit thinking about him so much, to quit wondering . . .

Ms. Hardigree's eager voice put any further doubts to rest. "Taylor," she said anxiously, "you really should have told him yourself. He wasn't at all pleased to hear the news from me. Remember what you said once about the icewater in his veins? Well, the icewater's boiling."

Taylor swallowed nervously. "Oh?"

Ms. Hardigree continued, in a soothing tone. "I had to warn you, dear. I think he's on his way over to see you."

Taylor sent a horrified glance to Nita. "On his way here? Yes, Ms. Hardigree. Yes, of course I forgive you. No, don't worry, I'll explain it to him."

Taylor replaced the receiver with a shaking hand and stood to face Nita. She felt the color draining from her face. "Kayne found out about my trip. He'll be here any minute."

Nita's eyes danced with excitement. "Not very happy with you, is he? Well, good for him! Come on kids, we'd better scram."

Taylor's stomach churned with cold dread. "Nita, you're not leaving me! You can't leave me alone like this."

Dreadful images raced through her head, images of

Kayne at his angriest, when his eyes were their bluest, smoldering like two glittering gemstones in a raging fire. "Nita," she murmured weakly, "you don't know what he's like when he's angry!"

Nita smiled in appreciation. "I can well imagine! Really, Taylor, if I wasn't happily married myself, I might be just a little bit jealous of you." She stopped and shook her head. "But probably not. I like you too much. I have to admit, you deserve everything you're going to get!"

"Nita! How can you say that? He's going to come over here and . . . well, you don't know what he's going to do!"

Nita laughed, bustling her children out the door. "Mmm, I have a pretty good idea. Say good-bye to Taylor, kids."

Katie, Lily and Josh filed out the door, smiling in response to their mother's sudden change in mood, as if they too guessed that something funny was about to happen.

"Little traitors," Taylor muttered under her breath, shutting the door behind them. "That's what comes of spoiling children with too much ice cream. The sugar goes to their brain and suddenly, they turn on you."

She cleared the dishes from the kitchen table, still mumbling to herself, her mind reeling and unfocused. Kayne was on his way over. He was very angry. And she couldn't think of a thing to do.

At the possibility of confronting him, Taylor's brain had switched to automatic, her mind unable to deal with the daunting prospect. She didn't know whether to laugh or cry, to scream or—a loud knock sounded at her door—to *run*.

It was far too late for escape. The insistent pounding demanded to be heard.

"Open the door, Taylor."

She cringed, hesitating. Why, oh why, did these things *always* happen to her?

"Let me in, Taylor!"

She leaned against the door, silently willing him to go away and leave her in peace.

"Now!" Kayne's voice ordered in his most authoritative, most unrelenting tone. This was no calm, caring physician, but a hard-as-steel surgeon, a man used to being obeyed. "Immediately," he added in a low growl, "or I'll break the bloody door in!"

With trembling hands, Taylor threw back the bolt. Kayne didn't wait for an invitation. He pushed his way in, stepping swiftly inside, and slammed the door behind him. Within the space of a minute, his acute, searching gaze had taken in the suitcase by her bedroom door, the half-filled makeup case, the folded clothes piled neatly on her bed—all guilty evidence of her intentions. His bitter, accusing eyes focused on Taylor. "So, it's true. You are leaving."

She tried to avoid his painful, burning stare, tried to look away, but the power of his gaze was riveting. "Yes, I—I'm taking a vacation."

Kayne gave her a disbelieving glare. "I think there's more to it than that."

She looked down at the floor. "I don't know what you mean."

Kayne shook his head and folded his arms across

his chest, making the jagged scar on his hand look paler, more pronounced, in fascinating contrast to his sun-darkened skin. "I tried to find you at the hospital to tell you about Mitzy."

Taylor reached out to him. "About Mitzy? Kayne, is she all right? What about her?"

He took her hand and gave it a quick squeeze. "I heard from Bradington, the hospital we sent her to for further treatment. She's fine, recovering beautifully, in fact. They say her spirits are exceptionally good, thanks to the bear by her side."

Taylor let out a long sigh. "I'm so relieved to hear it. Kayne, thank you for telling me."

He frowned. "I tried to tell you at the hospital, but your *replacement* in the gift shop informed me you'd be gone for some time."

Taylor swallowed hard. "Well—"

"Then Ms. Hardigree told me about this . . . vacation. If you really were planning to take a vacation, I didn't understand why you would try to keep it a secret." He gave her a dark, shaken look. "Then I realized there must be something," he paused to take a deep breath, "or *someone* you're trying to run away from." He let his eyes stray back to the luggage. "Just how long do you plan to be gone, Taylor?"

Taylor turned away, unable to meet the hurt look in his eyes. "I've done what I can at Stuart General," she whispered, her voice barely audible to her own ears. "It's time to move on. I plan to resign in two weeks."

Kayne's voice sounded behind her, soft and incredulous. "I thought you cared more than that."

"I do care," she responded quietly, turning back to

him. She wanted to take him by the shoulders and shake him like crazy, to explain how that was precisely the problem. She cared too much.

"And yet, you're willing to leave it all behind? To give up without trying any harder?"

She gave him a puzzled stare. "But I have tried, Kayne. I've tried every way I can think of to give the patients what they need. But I have to think of myself now. I have to think of my own——" She'd been about to say "my own happiness", but somehow, the words seemed ridiculous. She doubted she'd ever be happy again. It wasn't just her happiness that was at stake, but her heart and soul, her very sanity.

"I wasn't speaking of the patients," Kayne said quietly. "I was talking about us."

"Oh," she murmured, at a sudden loss for words.

Kayne took a step toward her and pulled her into his arms. He stared intently down at her. "Did you think I'd let you go without saying good-bye?"

Taylor blinked, and to her complete dismay, a tear escaped from the corner of her eye and rolled defiantly down one cheek.

Kayne wiped it gently away. "It seems to me, Taylor Berne, that you're just as stubborn as ever. Just as maddeningly, attractively troublesome. Your lips tell me one thing," he dropped a soft kiss on her mouth, "and your eyes tell me another."

Taylor wasn't sure what her eyes were saying, but her lips were singing with joy, and her heart was crying in pain. How could a simple good-bye be so exquisitely sweet and so excruciatingly sad, all at the same time?

Kayne sighed heavily, stroking her cheek. "It's always been this way between us, hasn't it? You're the one complication I've never been able to solve. Ever since that first meeting in Ms. Hardigree's office, I knew you were going to be trouble.'' He laughed softly under his breath. ''If I'd only known how much.''

Her pride wounded, Taylor shot him a scathing glance. ''You haven't been exactly trouble-free yourself.''

He raised his eyebrows in some amusement. ''No? Well, maybe not, but I did manage to steer clear of disaster. Until I met you, that is.''

Taylor stiffened, sniffing back the tears. ''Well, at least I didn't intimidate everyone out of their wits, stalking the hospital halls like some mechanical medicine man.''

Kayne only laughed at her unflattering portrayal. ''An 'operating robot' is what you once called me, I believe. And a very accurate description it was.''

Taylor eyed him suspiciously. ''Well, what do you expect me to call someone who works himself silly and walks around all wired up with evil electronic gadgets?'' She stared pointedly at the beeper attached to his belt.

''Ah, yes, the pager,'' he said softly. ''Well, I'm afraid you're going to have to get used to that. You see, I can't very well get along without it.'' He paused, then added quietly, ''Or without you.''

Disconcerted, Taylor looked away to hide her confusion ''I—I don't know what you mean.''

Kayne shook her gently. ''Don't turn away from me, Taylor. It's time to face the facts. It's time to admit that we belong together, you and I.''

Taylor swallowed hard, barely comprehending the words. ''Together?''

Kayne nodded solemnly. ''It's inevitable, my darling, the only way I can think of to solve the 'complication'. You see, I made a very interesting discovery—I have a heart condition that isn't in any of my medical textbooks. A condition that's totally and completely incurable. I've discovered I love you, Taylor.''

''Oh, dear,'' she whispered.

He smiled faintly. ''It's true, I'm afraid, a very serious ailment. And there's only one way to alleviate it.'' He covered both of her hands in his and still smiling, looked down into her eyes. ''Marry me.''

Taylor's voice deserted her. Her heart was too full, too happy, to allow her to speak. How could she put such euphoric feelings into words?

Taking her momentary silence for hesitation, Kayne made another attempt to convince her. ''It's the beeper, right?'' he prompted. ''You don't think you could live with it?'' He unclipped the pager from his belt. ''I swear I'll only use it when I'm on call. And I'm not on call now.'' He tossed it lightly across the room. ''So much for modern technology. Taylor, I'd give up electricity if you asked me to. Only, please say 'yes.' ''

Taylor found her voice again. ''Yes!'' she said, laughing and crying simultaneously. ''Yes, I'll marry you!''

Kayne picked her up and spun her around the room. ''You had me worried there for a minute, Doc Berne. You almost had to resuscitate me on the spot. But it would've taken more than a simple 'no' to keep me away.''

He set her down gently and, brushing a stray lock

of hair from her face, stared into her eyes. "You taught me a lesson, Taylor—to trust in my own feelings. I finally realized that I am human, after all. Some things really are out of my control. Things like life and death and," he gave her a wry smile, "falling in love."

Taylor closed her eyes and rested her head on his shoulder, happier, more peacefully content than she'd ever been in her life. "I love you, Kayne."

He stroked the soft mass of her hair and held her close, held her as if he'd never let her go. "Were you really going to leave without telling me?"

She sighed, wondering if she would've had the strength to go through with it. "I had to. I couldn't go on seeing you without . . . without—"

He nodded in understanding. "It took me a while to admit it, but putting my own happiness on hold won't save any more patients. In fact, as a happily married man, I hope to be a better doctor."

Taylor smiled sweetly up at him. "And I promise to love, honor, and tolerate all beeping noises."

Kayne chuckled in appreciation. "Hopefully, that won't be necessary too often. With a little compromising between us, I think I can adjust my work schedule to make room for a wife," he paused as his grin grew even wider, "and a family."

Taylor's heart leapt at the warm promise in his eyes. Kayne wanted children! She could almost see them now, climbing into their father's lap on Sunday mornings, dragging their Teddy bears along with them. Patches would be there too, curled up by the great picture window, watching the river for signs of jumping fish.

Kayne exhaled slowly. "With a wife who looks like

that when she smiles, I'm afraid it's going to be very difficult to go to work some mornings."

She laughed, then lowered her eyes, suddenly shy. Between the two of them, they would manage to juggle the demands of work and family. The magic of love made all things possible. "Kayne, I'm only sorry we won't be working together anymore. It really is too bad there isn't any money for 'Bear Care'."

He held her at arm's length, scratching his chin. "Well, that's not *exactly* true."

Taylor frowned, confused. "It isn't?"

Kayne drew her over to the couch and started to explain. "I've been busy over the past few days, drumming up interest in your bears."

She wrinkled her brow, still puzzled. "But the Board said—"

"This isn't about the Board," Kayne told her. "It's something I've been working on independently. It concerns the respiratory therapy bear we developed."

Taylor widened her eyes. "What about it?"

"I've spoken to a few of my colleagues at other hospitals. I explained the bear to them and the basic principle behind it." He paused, smiling. "They're very enthusiastic about the idea. . . . "

Taylor stood up from the couch, unconsciously propelled by the exciting news. "That's wonderful!"

Kayne caught her hands in his and drew her back down to him. "I hope you're able to maintain that eagerness of yours. In a few months you may not feel so delighted about it."

She regarded him with some surprise. "What makes you say that?"

Kayne's smile grew slightly apologetic. ''Well, the other doctors were so enthusiastic they wanted to purchase their own respiratory bears immediately—''

''Kayne, you didn't—''

''I did,'' he confessed. ''I took orders for more than a hundred of them.''

Taylor's jaw dropped, but after a moment's thought, she started to grin herself. ''Kayne, it's so simple. I can put the profit we make back into the 'Bear Care' program.''

He nodded. ''I was hoping you'd feel that way.''

She laughed, and threw her arms around him in a great bear hug. ''A perfect prescription, Dr. Frost.''

''Hmm,'' he muttered, holding her tight. ''It seems I won't be the only member of this family who's going to be overworked.'' He pulled back, eyeing her with concern. ''Do you think you're up to the job?''

She smiled up at him. ''As long as I get time off every now and then. Time to spend with my husband,'' she added softly.

He leaned nearer and brushed his warm lips against hers. ''I'll insist on it. In fact, time off with me is the most important part of your job. I plan to start with a month-long honeymoon.''

Taylor took a long, breathless minute to properly return his kiss. Then with a teasing look in her eyes, she held her hand to his forehead to check for outward signs of fever. ''A month off!'' she exclaimed. ''Dr. Frost, are you ill?''

Kayne didn't answer, only drew her closer for another kiss. Seconds later, Taylor's suspicions were confirmed. Dr. Frost's temperature was way above normal.